LAMB

LAMB

Bernard MacLaverty

Chivers Press • Thorndike Press
Bath, England   Thorndike, Maine USA

This Large Print edition is published by Chivers Press, England, and by Thorndike Press, USA.

Published in 1999 in the U.K. by arrangement with Random House (UK) Limited.

Published in 1999 in the U.S. by arrangement with International Creative Management.

U.K. Hardcover   ISBN 0–7540–3475–5 (Chivers Large Print)
U.K. Softcover   ISBN 0–7540–3476–3 (Camden Large Print)
U.S. Softcover   ISBN 0–7862–1609–3 (General Series Edition)

The text of this Large Print edition is unabridged.
Other aspects of the book may vary from the original edition.

Set in 16 pt. New Times Roman.

Printed in Great Britain on acid-free paper.

British Library Cataloguing in Publication Data available

Library of Congress Cataloging-in-Publication Data

MacLaverty, Bernard.
    Lamb / Bernard MacLaverty.
       p.   cm.
    ISBN 0–7862–1609–3 (lg. print : sc : alk. paper)
    1. Catholic Church—Ireland—Clergy—Psychology—Fiction.
2. Christian Brothers—Ireland—Fiction. 3. Kidnapping—
Ireland—Fiction. 4. Boys—Ireland—Fiction. 5. Large type
books. I. Title.
[PR6063.A2474L3   1998]
823'.914—dc21
                                      98–35738

To the memory of my father

CHAPTER ONE

There were things at the bottom of Brother Sebastian's bag that he didn't know were there. He was just unpacking when there was a knock on the door and the boy Higgins said that Brother Benedict would see him in his room as soon as he was ready. Brother Sebastian shaved quickly in cold water because, with all the fuss, he had not had time that morning. Then, in the late light of the evening, he went along to the Superior's room.

'Come in,' called Brother Benedict. He was stooping over, poking the fire, and when Brother Sebastian went in he turned short-sightedly to see who it was.

'Ah, Brother Sebastian. It's you. Sit down.'

Brother Sebastian was tall and broad-shouldered. His hair was slightly longer than Brother Benedict would have preferred it to be.

The room was shelved from floor to ceiling with books. There were piles of books on the table and the desk and a pile stood precariously on a small set of library steps.

Brother Sebastian sat while the fire was raked of its dead ash and new black turfs built into a pyramid. A yellow flame burned up.

'It must have been a trying time for you,' said Brother Benedict. 'I know what it can be like. You look drawn. I keep a little something for an emergency such as this.'

He rattled deep in a cupboard and produced a bottle of Power's.

'Will you take it alone—or with water?'

'With plenty of water, please,' said Sebastian, smiling.

'When I indulge I take it neat. It's the only way.'

Brother Sebastian wondered what was wrong. He had never been treated like this before by Benedict. He was after something. Brother Benedict poured Sebastian a whiskey but refused to have one himself.

'Well, how are things? How did the funeral go?'

'Not so bad, considering.'

'You'll forgive my appearance.' Brother Benedict indicated himself with inturned fingers. Over his soutane and white collar he wore a plastic apron with a large bottle of Guinness on it. He picked up a purple feather duster and began to wave it around. 'But I've decided once and for all to catalogue my books. *You* don't have much call for them do you, Brother? In the woodwork room. Skills of the hand rather than the mind.'

'No.'

'I decided a long time ago to specialize. Latin, Greek and Gaelic. You'll find nothing else among my books. I always say that a man with one language is like a man with one eye.

2

Now I myself have four good eyes and a few lesser ones—which could be polished up, as it were. Like glass eyes—not much use but presentable.' He laughed aloud.

Brother Sebastian smiled for him.

'Just wait till I finish this one and I'll be with you,' said Benedict. He took a book from the library steps, dusted it thoroughly then wrote a number in white ink at the base of the spine. He blew on the ink to dry it. Then he wrote something on to filing cards he had on his desk. He put the book on the shelf and moved the rest to the table.

'I bought this little lot on the Quays in Dublin—oh, it must be thirty years ago. They were second-hand before you were born.' He smiled at them. He lifted his soutane at the knees and sat on the library steps. The toecaps of his black shoes were burnished and reflected the light from the fire. He lit a cigarette.

'Was there any trouble in the Six Counties when you were home?'

'No. That was the last thing I was thinking about.'

'Yes, I'm sure,' said Brother Benedict. 'But, you know, it's something we should keep at the front of our minds. If in our position we can't be seen to help, then we should not stand in their way. They are angry men with vision, Brother, and by God their anger is justified. Ireland has not much longer to suffer. Her

3

misery will soon be over and we'll be a united country again.'

'Yes,' said Brother Sebastian, 'but I don't like their methods.'

'Nor do I, Brother. Nor do I. But do you like the methods of the British Government any better?'

'No.'

'For one thing, the propaganda machine they have. The whole of the Press is totally behind them. They make our men of vision out to be thimbleriggers and cornerboys. A ragged army of louts. Do you think louts could harass the might of Britain for so long?'

Brother Sebastian shrugged and sipped his whiskey. Brother Benedict was on one of his themes again. It was obvious that Brother Sebastian did not want to become involved in an argument, but the old man went on.

'I'll admit that every organization has its share of rogues. Even in the Brothers you'll find them. But we can't tar them all with the one brush. You're an Ulsterman. You should know the truth of the situation. What do you think?'

Asked such a direct question by his Superior, Brother Sebastian felt he had to answer.

'You describe them as men of vision . . .'

'I do. I do indeed.'

'But human elements can't be kept out. Anger, hatred spoil the purity of the vision and

4

the result is evil. If you know anyone who was killed then you know how evil it is.'

'In the course of history we cannot mourn individuals, Brother. That may seem harsh but it is true. Who mourns for the innocent of the French Revolution? Anybody?'

Brother Sebastian refused to answer but sat staring at his feet, hoping that the conversation would end. He had had a hard three days since his father's death and only now was it beginning to sink in. Brother Benedict must have noticed his reluctance because he changed the subject.

'Are there any relatives left at home?'

'No. I was an only child and my mother died years ago.'

'Your father was a good man—and immensely proud of you the day of your final vows. He and I had a long chat that day. He told me of the joy he felt that a son of his should be devoting his life to the Church. He said that it made his life worthwhile.'

'Yes, I knew.'

'The priesthood, he said, would have put too much responsibility on you. He admired your humility. What was it that . . .?' Brother Benedict waved the feather duster vaguely and it was the tone of his voice that asked the question.

'The doctor said that he died of a perforated ulcer. They found him with his rosary in his hands and a bottle of Milk of Magnesia on the table. He never knew he had an ulcer.'

'Sad. Sad.'

In the fire the damp turf spat a bit and hissed quietly, Brother Sebastian waited for the next question. The whiskey was hot in his throat.

'Forgive my asking, but did he die intestate?'

'Sorry?'

'Intestate.'

'I don't know what that means.'

Brother Benedict rolled his eyes to heaven and said in a voice that was not meant to be cutting,

'I am surrounded by the Educationally Sub-Normal. Did he die without leaving a will?'

Brother Sebastian hesitated. He thought he saw now the reason for the fire building and the substantial whiskey. He drank it off.

'He left a will and, as far as I know, everything goes to me.'

'Ah, good,' said Benedict. The long white ash of his cigarette dropped on to his soutane and he flicked it off with the duster. 'Finance can be so difficult. These are hard times, Brother. Do you know, it has often occurred to me that we should have the boys neutered. Look what we would save in laundry bills.'

Brother Sebastian failed to make the connection and did not laugh.

'The sheets, man, the sheets.'

He smiled because he knew the elder man wanted him to. Brother Benedict said,

'Can I tell you a little story against myself? Do you mind?'

Brother Sebastian said that he didn't.

'Well, the last time I was up in Dublin I was requiring a hair-cut—like somebody else I'll not mention—and I found myself in one of these ... these ... How shall I say it in English? One of these "modern joints" with female hairdressers. They set me down with this sheet around my neck and summoned this fine-looking lassie to cut my hair. I was looking at her in the mirror when, to cut a long story short, she banged me over the head with the brush and ran away.' He waited for an interested question from Brother Sebastian.

'Why?'

'She thought I was abusing myself.'

'What?'

'I knew that would get you. I had been cleaning my glasses beneath the sheet to get a better look at her—like so,' he moved his finger and thumb up and down slowly and rhythmically, 'and she had seen the sheet moving and me watching her. When the manager took off the sheet and saw me—in clerical dress—cleaning my specs and the lassie at the back of the shop crying her eyes out there was all hell let loose. She got the sack for having a filthy mind.'

'That's disgusting.'

'I know. There's no telling the dirty minds people have.'

Brother Sebastian's face was wrinkled in distaste. There was silence between them.

'You're not fit to live in the world, Brother. You think yourself too good for it?'

Brother Sebastian did not reply. Brother Benedict stared at the younger man and said,

'You strike me as the sort of person who is witty in retrospect—in the quiet of your room afterwards.'

'How do you mean?'

'Well, it's just that you never say anything witty when you're with me—and I always like to think the best of people.'

He lit another cigarette from a red piece of turf he picked up with a long pair of tongs.

'Had your father a big farm?'

'No. There's not much money—if that's what you mean.'

'Approximately.'

'Once all the debts are paid there will be very little.'

Brother Benedict took his empty glass and refilled it.

'Nevertheless. Every little helps. The Brothers are sorely in need of it this weather.'

'The Brothers?'

'Yes. Your vow of poverty. You remember?'

'I'm sorry, I just wasn't thinking.'

'Yes, I'm sure you're upset after these last few days.'

The whiskey was beginning to make Brother Sebastian's head light. He hadn't eaten since

8

he left home at midday. He didn't know whether it was the whiskey or the sight of the man sitting opposite him or the emotional strain of his father's death that made him do it but, before he could stop himself, he said,

'I'm thinking of leaving.'

When he said it he was amazed. He hadn't even voiced the thought aloud to himself. It had been there for a long time in the back of his mind but it had all seemed so difficult, the problems were so insuperable, that he never gave it any real consideration. Now that his father could no longer be hurt it seemed different, but that he should be saying it now to Brother Benedict of all people, left him slightly breathless. The statement hung in the air between them. Brother Benedict, with a gesture of the hand and a tilting of the head, turned it round and viewed it from different angles.

He got off the library steps, put away his feather duster and took off his Guinness apron. A Brother again, he sat down in his own chair and joined his hands. He said quietly,

'Freedom is an affliction, Brother. Now, who or what is tempting you to leave?'

Brother Sebastian moved awkwardly in his chair. Benedict sat waiting with a bird-like tilt of the head, sharp, beakish, owl-like. He tended to look with one eye, one side of his face, before he pecked.

'You couldn't have taken your vow of

9

poverty too seriously?'

'No, it's not that,' said Sebastian.

'Then what is it?'

Because Brother Benedict had taken what he said so calmly and because the whiskey had taken the edge off his usual wariness, he said,

'It's everything—everything about this place. What it stands for.'

'For instance?' His voice had gone thin, a chicken eyeing a seed.

Brother Sebastian groped for an example.

'Well, a place that can treat a twelve-year-old boy as a criminal for mitching school and running away from home. That can't be right?'

'Ah, we have favourites, do we? Young Owen Kane, isn't it? We shouldn't allow ourselves to become too attached to any one boy in particular. You know what that can lead to.'

'It was *you* who talked of dirty minds.'

'I shall ignore that remark, Brother. There is a distinct difference between realism and innuendo. And while we are on the subject, it has reached my ears that you *are* spending too much time with that boy.'

'But he needs a lot of time. Nobody has ever spent time on him before.'

'I admire your text-book idealism, Brother Sebastian, but I have rarely seen it work. You are being influenced by the tenderness of his years. Do you believe in the Church, Brother?'

'Yes.'

'Then you must believe that if a boy is old enough to receive communion he is old enough to break the law, to cause suffering in others.'

'But if they do not fully realize what they are doing . . .'

'Diminished responsibility, Brother, can only be claimed for babies, idiots and nuns.' He rose from his chair as if the meeting was at an end. The full skirt of his soutane blocked out the blaze of the fire.

'What we run here, Brother, is a finishing school for the sons of the Idle Poor.'

'It finishes them all right.'

Brother Benedict stopped in mid-flight, his eyebrows raised in mock pleasure.

'Ah. A witticism. You are not totally lost yet, Brother. I'll thank you not to interrupt me again. What we run here is a school for the sons of the Idle Poor. We teach them to conform, how to make their beds, how to hold a knife and fork, and the three Rs. We shoehorn them back into society at an age when, if they commit another offence, they go to the grown-up prison. If they do not conform we thrash them. We teach them a little of God and a lot of fear. It is a combination that seems to work. At least *we* think so. There is no room here for your soft-centred, self-centred idealism.'

'I think . . .'

'Your problem, Brother Sebastian, is that

you can't think. In all your time here I do not think I have heard you make a rational statement.'

'Brother Benedict, I . . .'

'You are overwrought, Brother. Like it or not, I am your spiritual father. You will join me on my walk every day next week.'

Benedict took his walk each day at the same time, summer and winter, selecting a different Brother to accompany him on a weekly rota. To get to know them informally, he said. At moments of crisis, Brothers like Sebastian were required to jump the queue. He rose unsteadily to his feet. Benedict said,

'And remember, if you do leave in hurried circumstances we can make it difficult for you to get a job. The Church in Ireland, Brother, has as many fingers as there are pies. Remember that.'

Brother Benedict held the door open for him to go out.

Once outside he walked the lino-covered, Lysol-smelling corridor with his fists knotted. He stopped, then turned on his heel and walked back to the door. He knocked and Benedict opened it.

'Yes?'

'There are still some things to be cleared up at home and there is no one else to do it. Can I have permission to go back at the week-end?'

'If you must you must,' said Benedict and closed the door in his face.

CHAPTER TWO

'Some day, Brother Sebastian, I'm going to kill you,' said Owen. The boy sat on the sand opposite Brother Sebastian, staring with narrowed eyes into his face.

'All I said,' laughed Brother Sebastian, 'was that this is all you are good for. Minding the clothes. Provided there is no money in the pockets.' The boy sat handfulling sand and letting it trickle through his fingers.

'You don't trust me,' he said.

'You don't trust me either.'

The screams and whoops from the rest of the group floated to them from the water's edge. It was early in the morning and they were having the one bathe they were permitted each day.

'Just because I'm not allowed to swim . . .' said Owen.

'It's for your own good. God knows what would happen to you if you went in the water with your condition.'

The boy began pouring sand from one hand to the other. He had nothing more to say. Brother Sebastian found talking to him difficult.

He had known Owen since he had first come to the Home about two years ago and, although the boy never told him much at a

13

time, he had managed to build up a picture of what his life had been like before. At the beginning he found it difficult to separate the truth from the lies.

Owen was from Dublin, from a large housing estate on the east side.

'It's like Ballymun—only it's rough,' was what he said about it. He had been put away because he had continually mitched school and had run away from home frequently—the Gardai had been informed on four occasions at least. God knows how many times they had not been. Since coming to the Home he had twice absconded.

Brother Sebastian hadn't taken to him right away, because he was not that sort of child, with his small furrowed face, but over his time at the Home he had grown to like him. He had attractive qualities of openness and resilience. What was more was that the boy seemed to seek Brother Sebastian out if he wanted anything, which he thought showed the beginnings of a trust. To achieve anything with these boys a trust was necessary.

He was the last of a family of five boys. The two eldest were in Mountjoy Jail (one of whom Owen had never seen at all), one was in the Merchant Navy and the sixteen-year-old had just joined the Free State Army. His father, if indeed it was his father, had been a lorry driver, away for weeks on end in England. When he came home he would get drunk and

14

whip Owen with whatever came to hand, a length of electrical flex, his belt, a bamboo cane, an old leather his own father used to sharpen his razor on. One night he came home with a piece of rubber hose pipe which he whistled through the air as a warning.

When he was at home he would inspect Owen's bed each morning, slipping his ice-cold hand beneath the boy. If Owen had wet the bed during the night he would take him and plunge him into a cold bath, sometimes even forcing his head underneath the water.

'This'll toughen you up, ya pissin' cissy,' he would shout as he did it.

Then one day he went away. He went on a driving job to England and never came back. Brother Sebastian asked the boy if he was glad when this happened and he had replied that it made no difference. He was afraid that he would come back any day. The door would just open and he would be there.

The only person Owen spoke of with anything approaching affection was his grandmother, his mother's mother. He would go sometimes and stay with her and she would get drunk and give him money and hug him and call him 'lamb'. He would light the fire for her and do her messages. He always tried to short-change her but she was not to be fooled. Owen demonstrated how she would hold the coins up to the level of her chin and move her lips, then say,

15

'You're 10p short, Owney.'

For some reason she always called him Owney. She wore men's socks in bed and every night that Owen slept with her she set the alarm clock for seven thirty, even though she never got up before midday.

His mother he rarely spoke of.

And yet he preferred all that to living in the Home. It was miles from nowhere on a promontory jutting its forehead into the Atlantic wind. If a boy absconded he had to walk about ten miles of peat bog, if he wanted to avoid being picked up on the road, before he reached another route.

It was a big house 'from the days of the British Occupation', as Brother Benedict said with a curl of his lip. Over the years bits had been added on here and there. Within the house itself stone flags would give way to brown lino, showing the seam of the extensions. The walls were painted throughout a pale hospital green above shoulder level, and below, a dark hospital green. The only remnant of better days was the ornamental plaster ceilings. The stables had been made into a chapel. Brother Benedict had said that it gave him some satisfaction to see a pagan British stable become converted to the Catholic Church. There were various prefabs scattered around the house for classrooms. Surrounding the whole complex was a high wire fence which screamed and whistled in the

16

constant wind from the sea. It seemed to rain continually.

The place was scrubbed and clean and dead—'like a corpse', as one of the boys put it. The air was full of disinfectant and polish and each boy had a cleaning duty to do every day.

Brothers, always on the alert, walked the corridors. In the grounds they moved like crows, their black soutanes flapping.

When he did talk, Owen's incessant theme was his hatred for the Home. He loathed the food and the Brothers (he would tell Brother Sebastian this and somehow in the telling Sebastian was excluded), especially Brother Benedict whom he feared almost as much as his father. He loathed the fact that he had a rubber sheet on his bed in the dormitory and that all the boys made fun of him because of it. 'Kane the Stain' they called him. He loathed the prayers and processions, the classes, the scrubbing, the wind and sea—everything about the place. Because he was younger than the others, he made few friends. He was a loner walking the perimeter wire.

He was glad now to be sitting out from the crowd with Brother Sebastian 'minding the clothes', even though there wasn't a person for ten miles to steal them.

'They said prayers for you in Chapel when you were away,' he said.

Brother Sebastian looked up.

17

'For me?'

'Well, for your . . . Dad.'

It was the first mention Owen had made of the death. Brother Sebastian flattened out an area of sand with his hand.

'Was he O.K. of a Dad?'

'Yes, he was good. We were good friends.'

'Friends? You weren't glad then?'

'No.'

Brother Sebastian squared off the ends of his plateau. He looked all around. The rest of the boys were still horsing about in the water. They wouldn't come until he called them.

'Did you ever think of running away again, Owen?'

For a moment the boy's eyes lit up and the furrows disappeared from his forehead. Then they came back again.

'Naw. It never works. I always get caught. I'm too wee to work or anything.'

'What would you say to me taking you away from this place?'

The boy considered this, not really understanding.

'You mean you and me?'

'Yes.'

'Are you on the level?'

'Yes. But I've got to arrange it first. Give me till the week-end. What do you say?'

'Yeah. Smashin'.'

'If you say anything to anybody, it's off. Anybody. I wouldn't want to take you against

18

your will, but if you stay here you will have no life. Nothing. Swear that you will say nothing to anyone.'

The boy nodded lest the sound he made would give it away. Brother Sebastian stood up and whistled the bathers back with two fingers.

*   *   *

Brother Sebastian, in plain clothes for the week-end, sat on a hard creaking chair outside the solicitor's office waiting his turn. It was a passageway rather than a waiting room. Some magazines, years out of date, lay around on the seats. Brother Sebastian leafed through them. *Woman, Home Beautiful, Boys' Own, The Economist.* He folded his arms and looked at the ceiling. Still the voices droned on from inside the office. He read the jokes page in *Boys' Own* and laughed to himself. He got up and went to the end of the passage and looked out of the window into the street of the small Ulster market town. He knew almost every face going in and out the shops, although now he had to struggle to remember some of the names. Women gossiped and a dog walked sideways across the street. The bus came in and bounced a tied pile of morning newspapers off the pavement. Brother Sebastian went back to his seat.

The office door opened and Maguire came out with an old lady. He showed her to the stairs and told her to be careful because the handrail was broken. He turned to Brother Sebastian and invited him into the office.

'I never know whether to call you Brother Sebastian or Michael Lamb.'

'I think Michael Lamb is best for business,' he said, smiling.

'Righty-ho. What can I do for you, Michael?'

Maguire was young and immaculately dressed in contrast to his grubby office. He drove a brand new sports car and everybody said he was raking it in. Michael hesitated, cleared his throat and began.

'I was wondering if there was any way to speed up this will business. I would like to know whether I owe people money or I'm going to get money.'

'Righty-ho. Let's see now.' He went to a filing cabinet and took some papers out and plucked a silver biro from his inside pocket. As he worked he licked his bottom lip with a stiff tongue. 'Well, you'll be glad to know, Michael, that you don't owe any money.'

'Good,' said Michael. 'Can you tell me how much there is?'

'Not exactly, at the moment. But I would say it wouldn't be a kick on the arse off two thousand. If you'll excuse my French, Brother.'

'And when is the earliest I can get it?'

'Let me see now.' Maguire leaned back in his chair, drumming his biro on the papers. 'About three months?'

'Oh,' said Michael. 'That's far too long.'

'It's the way the law grinds, Brother.'

Michael sat, not knowing what to say next.

'Did you want the money urgently? What for, might I ask?'

'It's sort of personal.'

Maguire laughed again.

'Ask me no questions and I'll tell you no lies. Eh?'

'That's it.'

'It's not a shady deal, is it?'

Michael was too slow in answering.

'No,' he said.

'I get the picture. I know more than you think, Michael.' He assumed the attitude of a conspirator, his face doing all but winking.

'Righty-ho,' he said. 'I can let you have something in advance. But be warned. I have to charge dearly for it. If I put my neck in a noose it'll cost you. Righty-ho?'

Michael moved to the edge of his seat and sighed with relief.

'How much can you let me have?'

'Eight hundred. It's all I have on the premises at the moment.' He went to a small steel safe in the corner and opened it with a key. He took out a brown envelope and handed it to Michael.

'You may check it if you wish.'

Michael counted the ten-pound notes, wetting his finger. He had never seen so much money in his life. He felt a guilty elation as he reached the last one.

'Let me have your signature. Here,' Maguire said. The silver biro felt like ice in his hand as he signed.

'Remember that this is just between ourselves, Michael. I'm doing you a favour. Best to speak to no one about it. Righty-ho?'

Michael nodded and rose to go. Maguire leaned back in his chair expansively. He said,

'I had a call from a Brother Benedict the other day.'

'What?'

'Yes, I thought that might interest you. But I said that I would prefer to see you first before discussing any business.'

'Thank you very much, Mr Maguire. You did the right thing.'

'Thank *you*, Michael. Any time I can be of assistance.'

They shook hands and Michael left, holding tightly on to his bulging envelope.

CHAPTER THREE

The tide had withdrawn almost completely, leaving the sand of the beach flat, except for where stones and other débris stood. Here the sand had been hollowed out on the seaward side in the shape of a plunging comet's tail. The same pattern had formed round washed-up jelly-fish, with their delicate lilac traceries of innards. The Atlantic roared continuously on to the rocks at the point.

At four o'clock the two Brothers in buttoned black soutanes moved across the beach. They had come from the Home, set like a fortress on the cliff above the point. They walked the hard flat sand, talking.

'Obedience, Brother, is a very rare virtue,' said Brother Benedict. 'Simple people have it—and it tends to go hand in hand with humility. Don't you agree?'

Brother Benedict had his hands behind his back, watching the sand directly in front of his feet. Outside, in the light, Sebastian thought he looked much older. He agreed with him about obedience and humility, while avoiding meeting his eye directly. Sebastian stared ahead but from the corner of his eye was aware of Benedict watching him. The older man always set the pace for their walk and Sebastian had, occasionally, to skip a few quick steps to keep up with him.

'I once knew a young Brother who fancied himself as a calligrapher,' Benedict rolled the word off his tongue with obvious pleasure, 'and one night he was writing a text with the word "obedience" in it. He had just begun the letter O when I called him, and he came to me immediately. Do you know, when I went into his room I saw that he had not even taken time to close the letter O. *That* is what I call obedience.'

Brother Benedict turned to him and smiled. He stopped walking and asked,

'Do you believe that, Brother?'

Sebastian felt uncomfortable. He shrugged his shoulders and raised his eyebrows.

'Why shouldn't I?'

'Yes, why shouldn't you?' Brother Benedict started walking again. 'As I said, it is a virtue associated with simple people. You should not have so much difficulty with it.'

'Oh but I do, Brother. It is most unnatural. When you can see it as the will of God it is easy. But sometimes . . .'

'Yes?'

'Sometimes it is difficult to see the will of God.'

'Like Abraham?'

Sebastian nodded.

'Abraham's problem,' said Benedict, 'was that he saw the will of God *too* clearly. The way an Ulster Protestant would—and that frightens me.'

Sebastian held back, not wanting to get involved in the same old arguments again. Benedict avoided a jelly-fish, taking an extra long stride.

The sun was bright and the two men cast shadows which rippled along over the ribbed sand closer to the water's edge. Sebastian felt uncomfortable and knew that he was perspiring under his clerical black. The silence

24

between them was awkward. Benedict reached the small flat arcs of the waves, hitched up the skirts of his soutane revealing a pair of blue flip-flops on his feet, and paddled in.

'Aaaahhh,' he said. ''Tis as warm as tea.'

He stood, his back to Sebastian, facing out to sea. His legs were thin and white, disappearing into the black skirt of his soutane. When he spoke Brother Sebastian moved round to hear him better. Sebastian wore black socks and sandals and kept having to jump back from the incoming ripples. Brother Benedict said,

'It's from *The Sayings of the Fathers*.'

'What is?'

'The story of the unclosed O. It didn't happen to me. Have you read the Fathers?'

'No.'

'Oh yes, I forgot. You don't read—English.'

Sebastian was making marks in the sand with the outside edge of his sandal. It raised fine furrows with a scuffing sound.

'Do you read French?' called Benedict. 'Brother Sebastian?'

'You know I don't.'

'A man with one language is like a man with one eye,' said Benedict seaward.

'What?' said Sebastian, moving to one side to hear him. A wave covered his left foot and he hopped out of the water to keep his other foot dry. Brother Benedict turned and came out of the water.

'They teach you young men nothing nowadays,' he said, dropping his soutane over his legs. 'Too much useless psychology.'

He was a tall thin man with black circular horn-rimmed glasses long out of fashion. His face seemed carved to the bone. His white hair was tufted and short and all of it still there. One particular tuft sat up at the crown of his head like a cockatoo. When he turned quickly it trembled. He stood in his proper element breathing deeply, filling his lungs with the salt sea air and exhaling it harshly. When he had taken twenty of these breaths they walked back up the beach, Benedict's feet making clicking noises in his plastic sandals.

They went back to the Superior's room and Sebastian had to stand and listen while Benedict talked.

'Can you swim, Brother Sebastian?'

'Yes, I taught myself. Can you?'

'Ah, self-taught?' Brother Benedict was drying his feet thoroughly, separating the toes like a hand of playing cards and carefully drying between each of them. 'Myself, ankle-deep is all I'm fit for, thank God,' he said. 'If I'm lost at sea I'll be spared the agonies of suffering. It was part of the Roman curriculum, you know. Reading, writing and swimming. I have tended to concentrate on the first two to the detriment of the third. In this matter I bow to your superiority.' He put both white feet on the carpet, not flat, but angled so that he could

26

inspect them properly. Then he reached into a drawer of his desk and produced a large pair of scissors and began cutting his toenails.

'But I must admit that the salt water—in small doses—is good for the whole system.'

A chip of nail ricocheted off the desk in Sebastian's direction. 'I'm sorry about that,' said Benedict, 'I should really borrow your secateurs for this job. The nails tend to get horny with age.' He looked up and smiled. 'Like celibates.'

Sebastian said quickly, 'You had something you wanted to discuss with me?'

Another fragment of nail winged past him.

'Ah, yes. But there is plenty of time for that. Once you've got over this phase of yours,' said Benedict.

Sebastian watched him shake talcum powder between his toes, tapping the tin with one finger. He pulled on a pair of clean grey socks.

'What I would like to know is how related this phase of yours is to your father's death, God rest his soul. I have just been reading Tacitus again,' he said, waving his hand towards the open book on the desk. 'He says of his father-in-law *"Felix opportunitate mortis"*. Is this the case for you?'

Sebastian looked at him blankly. Benedict sighed.

'It means "lucky or fortunate in the timeliness of his death". Did your father die just as your doubts came to the surface or had you been waiting for him to die?'

'I don't know.'

'Then I suggest you think about it. I also suggest you try to spend some time considering the nature of obedience. And above all, Brother Sebastian, I urge you to spend some time on your knees in prayer for guidance on these matters. Discover what is tempting you. Tomorrow I will speak to you further.'

For the first time since the interview began Sebastian smiled. For tomorrow, he had different plans.

*　　　*　　　*

It was a beginning of a sort. How long it would last Michael was unsure. Nevertheless he felt that rising spirit in himself which he had felt before when he did not know what was over the brow of a hill but knew that it could not be all that bad.

He stood on the deck of the boat as it pulled away from the harbour, his elbows taking his weight on the wooden rail. The boat threshed through the soupy green water, skinning it with white wake. Seagulls with hard yellow eyes coasted alongside, not three feet from his head, not flying but gliding, occasionally shrugging their shoulders to keep pace. They seemed invisibly tied to the boat, towed by it, except when they cackled and screamed and

28

dived into the wake to pick up scraps and clumsily take off again.

He reached down to the boy standing beside him, whose chin was just clear of the rail, and put his arm on his shoulder.

'Can we afford any bread for these fellas? Eh, Owen?'

'Yeah,' said Owen. Michael could see that he was loath to leave his place at the crowded rail in case it should not be there when he came back.

'I'll get it. Don't worry,' said Michael. When they had boarded the boat Michael had decided to stay on the open deck just in case the boy should be sick. His bag was keeping their place on one of the wooden benches. He unzipped it and pulled out the clear-wrapped sandwiches. He peeled a triangle of bread from the top one and looked at it. He went back to the boy.

'These birds'll not die from the butter they've spread on this,' he said. He tore a wedge off the bread and gave it to the boy.

'Hold it up,' he said. 'Higher.'

The boy stood on tiptoe, his arm extended towards the flying seagull. The bird seemed to look over his shoulder with contempt at the offering then sidled nearer. Michael put his arms round the boy's waist and held him up, he offering the boy, the boy offering the bread, the gull ignoring both.

Then suddenly from nowhere, from the

slipstream of the bird, a black-headed gull streaked and in a flurry of grey wings pinched the bread. Owen screamed with fright and struggled to get down. His fingers were pressed into his mouth.

'It bit me. It bit me,' he yelled, his voice crammed with fingers. Michael laughed and put his arms round him.'

'Let me see. Where's the blood? Let me see.'

Owen held out his fingers, glistening where he had sucked them. They were trembling.

'You'll live,' he said.

'But it bit me, the bugger.'

'Shhh,' said Michael. The incident had created a small crowd and they were looking sympathetically at the boy and at the man hunkered beside him. An audience was the last thing that Michael wanted. People could remember the smallest snippets of information. A man and a blond-haired boy. On the boat. A seagull snatched bread from his hand.

'Come on,' said Michael and hustled the boy away from the interest. He thought it best to go downstairs, away from the crowd at the rail.

'It's not too bad. We might get a seat.'

He parted the crowd with his bag and Owen followed behind him. They saw an empty seat in the tea bar and moved into it. Out of the window Michael saw the last shoulder of Ireland slip past.

30

'Well, Owen, we're away.'

The boy nodded, his eyes bright and nervous, glittering rather than shining.

'Sit down and make yourself comfortable.'

'Yes, Dad.' The boy smiled and winked cheekily and Michael cuffed him lightly on the head.

'Don't overdo it,' he hissed. He gave Owen the money to get two cups of tea. The boy, obviously proud to be trusted, swaggered up to join the queue at the counter. He brought back two plastic beakers, yelping with the heat in his fingers. It was the colour of blood and tasted of iron. They had thimblefuls of milk which had to be torn open and they both spilled them. Owen took some sugar lumps from his pocket and offered one to Michael, which he refused. They were wrapped in twos and Michael watched the boy unwrap three packets and plonk the lumps in his tea. Owen watched the tiny procession of bubbles rising to the surface.

'That's six lumps of sugar,' said Michael.

'I can count.'

'You'll ruin your teeth.'

Owen widened his lips and clacked his teeth together the way a chimp does.

'They're O.K.'

'That's only because they don't give you much sugar in the Home.'

They half finished their tea and Owen began to yawn.

'Tired?'

'Naw.'

'Stretch out here anyway.'

Michael put his feet up on the facing window ledge and the boy settled down beside him, nuzzling beneath his arm.

They'd been up since first light that morning, and soon the boy was asleep, his mouth dropping open. Michael, not wanting to waken him, used his other arm to cover him with the tail of his anorak. He adjusted his protective arm and noticed again the glitter of his ring. He was conscious of the pressure it exerted on his finger and the unusualness of seeing it flash as he moved his hand. He still thought it a reasonable idea. Owen had agreed, but that didn't mean much because he agreed with most things Michael said.

Owen had waited outside the shop in Belfast, minding the bag, while he went into the jeweller's. A woman came quietly over the carpet to him.

'Can I help you, sir?'

'Yes, I'd like a wedding ring.'

'Any particular price range, sir?' she said, going behind the glass counter.

'Not *too* dear,' said Michael. He leaned on the counter and felt it warm beneath his hand. He peered down into its lit interior at the selection of rings, shining gold on scarlet satin. They were half sunk in the plush.

'Ladies' or gents'?'

'It's for myself,' said Michael. 'I lost mine

and I don't want my wife to know.'

The woman seemed to understand because she nodded sympathetically.

'Yes, we get a lot of that in here. But it's the sentiment that's important, isn't it? A ring's a ring. It's what it means. That's the point.'

The woman produced a tray of men's rings and set them on the counter. Michael felt a moment of panic when he realized that he either did not know or had forgotten which hand it went on. He knew it was the third finger and flexed them both, his hands hanging by his sides.

'Just look at those, sir, to see if there is anything that takes your fancy.'

She bustled into the back of the shop and came back with a device for measuring the size of his finger.

'See anything like it?'

'Like what?'

'Like your ring. The one you lost.'

Michael pored over the tray and made an 'Mmmmm' sound for effect. He was so unsure he felt he had to say,

'Not really.'

She produced another tray, saying that these were slightly more expensive.

'That's the one,' said Michael pointing to a gold ring with tiny flat facets.

'My favourite,' she said. 'Let me see your size.'

Still Michael was reluctant to commit

33

himself to offering his right or left hand. He waited, pretending to be engrossed in the ring, until he saw out of the corner of his eye the woman make a move towards his left. He extended his hand and, flicking her eye from his finger to the device, she selected a hole from those she fanned out and tried it round his finger.

'Is that comfortable?' she asked.

'It's a bit sharp at the edges.'

She smiled at him, then selected a ring of the type he had chosen.

'Try that,' she said, helping him fit it on his finger. Michael smiled and said,

'Till death us do part and all that.'

'For richer for poorer,' said the woman, joining in.

The ring fitted him well. He felt a foolish desire to look at himself in a mirror, as if it was a suit he was trying on. He looked over his shoulder and saw Owen staring at him through the window, his nose flattened against the glass.

'That one will do grand,' he said. 'How much?'

'That one is forty pounds.'

'Fine.'

'Do you want me to put it in a box, sir?'

Michael hesitated. She looked at him slyly.

'Can I suggest that you don't bother with the box, sir? If your wife were to find it you might have some explaining to do.'

'Yes, you're right,' said Michael. He smiled at her. He liked her becoming involved in his conspiracy, or what she thought was his conspiracy. And it made his own game seem doubly clever. With the ring still on his finger, he took out a bundle of notes and paid.

'Just up from Dublin for the day?' she said as she wrote out his receipt.

'No, not Dublin,' said Michael. 'Galway. I'm on holiday.'

'I could have sworn your accent was sort of Dublin,' she said, flicking over the page and checking that the blue carbon had come through.

'My parents were from Dublin. Maybe that's it.'

'Maybe.'

Outside Owen was standing, the bag between his feet, looking in the window.

'Look at those,' he said, pointing to a tray of digital watches. They were satin finished, stainless steel with square black faces. One had been fixed so that it flicked up the time every few seconds in its red computer figures.

'Did you ever have a watch?'

'Naw.'

'Would you like one of those?'

Owen didn't believe him, but Michael brought him into the shop and asked to see the watches. Owen's wrist was too thin for any of the watches in the window. The woman showed them a child's watch of roughly the same design and they took that one. Owen asked her if it was waterproof and she said of course it was.

'Time, Owen?' Michael asked when they were outside.

'Four thirty-two.'

The boy's arm was now up over his ear, the face of the watch black and dead. He was best to sleep because now that they were getting well out to sea the boat was beginning to heave and lurch, despite the sunlight outside. Michael's leg went numb. He would have to move. He lifted Owen's head and pushed his anorak underneath. The boy snorted and curled up into a smaller ball, even though he now had the whole seat to himself. Seeing that he still slept, Michael went to the bar to get himself a drink. He queued with others, changing his weight from foot to foot as the boat tilted. When he got his pint he drank an inch into it so that he could carry it without spilling to where Owen slept.

He sat in the recess of the window opposite the sleeping boy, his back to the sea, and looked at him. He was small for his age—he didn't look much more than nine—and curled up he looked like a baby. His hair was fair and his closed eyelids had the brown pigment that goes with lack of sleep. Michael tilted his head to one side to see the boy's face the right way up. Thin and sharp, the skin pulled over bones that seemed brittle. Once he had broken his

36

collar bone and had screamed almost to fainting when Michael had stupidly tried to take his pullover off over his head. When his eyes were closed there was no light about his face. It was a dead face, an old face in contrast to the child-like stature. The boy's nails were bitten so much that the round flesh of his fingertips swelled over them, and yet he had never noticed him biting them. Michael swirled the flat beer to a head and, as he drank, tilting the glass, he noticed a man sitting at the opposite side of the lounge staring at him. When their eyes met the man's eyes flicked away.

Over the next half hour, each time Michael's eyes strayed to the far side of the lounge the little man was watching him and each time the man looked away. He was unused to the feeling that he was doing something wrong. All his life he had been on the right side of the law. What he was doing now was right, but he knew that many wouldn't agree with him. No one, except himself, knew enough to make a judgment.

The whole system was totally unjust. He had tried to change it from within, tempering the law at every opportunity with his own warmth. Now the saving of an individual was more important than the law. Owen was more important. Michael may have been able to help to some extent boys who in the future would have come to the Home but he had given up that chance for something more complete. Besides he had also to save himself from the slack tide of his own life.

He looked at the state of Owen's clothes. Beneath his anorak the frayed denims and the sneakers split across the uppers ... London would be time enough to kit him out. Old clothes were good enough for travelling. In Belfast he had noticed that the boy's flies were burst, the zipper pinching the gap in the middle. Beneath, his underpants were the colour of putty. His elbow jutted through a hole in his maroon sweater.

It was this caring for the boy that Michael looked forward to. Dressing him well, not prissily, buying him things he had never had before, taking him places. Teaching him. He knew there was more than enough time to salvage him, this piece of jetsam. Sacrifice was what was required.

He had never really felt this way before. The feeling he had had for his parents was something born of respect and gratefulness. He was used to them being there and was never conscious of his feelings for them. Years ago he had experienced something approaching this feeling for a girl who served in a sweet shop beside his school. Her pony tail, her brown eyes, her smile which he thought she reserved especially for him.

But the time had been one of religious fervour, of self-denial, and all his love was channelled towards Jesus and Mary. His store of it was so meagre that it allowed for no tributaries. All the intensity of his early life was saved for that time he would spend on bended knees either in front of the tabernacle or before the pictures in his bedroom.

One was entitled 'Save me Lord!' It was a black and white print of Jesus walking on the water, His hand raised in benediction, His lightly bearded face full of love and pity. He was half turned towards Peter who was in the act of sinking, his chin arched upwards to avoid the water, his arms thrown wide in appeal. The whites of Peter's eyes blazed with fear. The sea was grey and jagged with waves, Christ's garment moulded to His body by the wind of the storm, His black hair flying. Once Michael had climbed on a chair to look with microscopic closeness at the picture. It was made up of tiny dots, shades of black and grey, close in some parts, widely spaced in others. The only place where there were no dots was in the white of Peter's eyes. It was nothing which produced that look of terror. That close to the picture, Michael had noticed that a film of dust had gathered on the inside of the glass.

The other picture was of Our Lady of Perpetual Succour. Very dark, it had the wooden pose of an icon and her head was wreathed in gold. She held the Christ Child in hands that were long and thin and seemed the wrong way round, right for left and left for right. They did not hold the Child but were placed against Him as He floated. Her face was turned to heaven and exuded a love that Michael had tried to imitate.

Owen made a noise. Michael looked down at him, and as he stared at him the boy's eyes opened. He wrinkled his nose.

'Hiya,' he said.

CHAPTER FOUR

Too tired to travel further, they stayed that night in the first hotel they came to in Stranraer. The man who had stared at them also checked in and, because they had travelled on the same boat, the man took the liberty of speaking to Michael.

'A nice crossing.'

'Yes, indeed.'

Michael was sitting in the small quiet bar before having a meal. Owen was outside wandering in the garden. The man arranged himself in a chair beside Michael.

'On holiday?' he asked.

'Yes.'

Michael was fascinated by his eyelids. He had never seen anything like them before. They looked as if they were oiled, two domes set beneath his eyebrows. His presence made him feel uneasy.

'Was that your boy with you today?'

'Yes,' said Michael.

'A good-looking boy.'

The man's voice was light and his cadences had the tinge of a woman in them. Michael wanted to get up and go but he didn't want to offend. The man introduced himself. He reached out his hand and shook Michael's. His hand lingered too long and made Michael's skin crawl.

'My name's Lamb, Michael Lamb. How do you do?'

Michael wondered if he should have given a different name but it was too late now.

'What do you do for a living?' the man asked.

'I'm a joiner by trade.'

'You look strong enough for it, anyway.'

Just then Owen came in through the door, followed by a waitress. His voice was excited.

'Tea's ready, Brother,' he said.

Michael got up and gave him a withering look. At table he said in a whisper,

'I'd just told that guy you were my son and you come in blabbing your mouth off all over the place, "Tea's ready, Brother". Brother! When the news gets out it'll not take him long to figure out who we are.'

Owen was hurt at being told off and ate in silence. Rather than meet the man again they went to their room for what was left of the evening.

*   *   *

The next morning at the train Michael was left carrying the bag while Owen rushed on ahead to get a window seat. They sat in the silence of the stopped train opposite one another and smiled.

'So far so good,' said Michael.

The carriage window faced a cement gable covered in graffiti, spray paint of different colours, chalk, gloss white which had run with a fringe of icicles. It had begun to rain, darkening the top half of the gable. Spits of rain quivered on the window pane.

'How do you like England?' Michael asked the boy.

'O.K. Anyway it's Scotland.'

'What's the farthest you've been from Dublin?'

The boy thought.

'I dunno. I think I was in Skerries once.'

Michael opened a can of Coke for him with a small explosion. The brown liquid frothed up and Owen put his mouth over the hole, sucking in the foam.

The gable wall moved and they were away. The countryside was grey-green in the rain. The drops now slashed horizontally across the window with the speed of the train. They did not speak except to say the names of the various stations they passed through. They had to go north to Glasgow, then as they moved south the sky cleared and the rain stopped. Owen found an ash tray at his elbow and began to click the flap up and down. He looked inside the aluminium lid, then flicked it louder and louder.

'Knock it off,' said Michael. The boy stopped.

'Any fags?' he asked.

The train stopped at Carlisle. Michael seemed annoyed. He leaned forward in his seat and spoke to the boy in a tight whisper.

'Look, how many times do I have to tell you? Not in public.'

His voice died away when a man, grunting with a heavy suitcase, stopped beside them. He slid his case between the backs of the seats, took off his overcoat and sat down. Michael knew that there would be no talk from Owen for as long as the man sat there. The boy was wary like an animal. Michael remembered when he came to the Home how he had flinched away if anyone near him made a quick movement. A scratch of the head and the boy would duck. Owen did not look at the man but Michael could see that he was annoyed. The boy stared out of the window and put his sneakers up on his seat, scuffing them about. His brow creased. Michael had never seen so many wrinkles in a child of his age.

The man sat puffing slightly. He was corpulent and when he stretched out his legs they saw he wore old-fashioned boots. The train shuddered and moved off from the darkness of the station into the brightness of the town. Roofs, back gardens, a queue of traffic, familiar shops with unknown names, a football field with one man in a blue track-suit, running. The fat man pulled out a packet of cigarettes and Michael saw Owen's eyes swivel to the side. The man lit one and inhaled. He coughed, turning red.

The train began to gather speed and Owen's fingers tapped in rhythm. The pale blue smoke drifted towards him and he wrinkled his nose. Then his hand dived into his pocket and he pulled out a sugar lump and tossed it into his mouth. It cracked and crunched as he chewed it with open mouth. The fat man looked down sideways at him. Owen brought out another two lumps and put them in his mouth, making the same noise.

The fat man leaned forward to Michael and said, nodding at the boy, 'We used to have a horse like that.'

Michael smiled at the man's joke.

'Did you remember to bring your tablets?'

The boy nodded.

'Take one now then.'

Owen took a tablet and a sugar lump and crunched them together, swilling them down with another Coke.

The fat man leaned across to Michael again and asked the way to the bar. Michael pointed.

The man heaved himself to his feet, stubbing a large cigarette end into the armrest ash tray and lumbered off up the train. Owen got up.

'Where are you going?' asked Michael.

'The john.'

'How many sugar lumps did you nick?'

The boy just smiled over his shoulder. As the boy moved past Michael he heard the click of the ash tray closing. He looked out the window. They were moving into the countryside again. The fields were huge compared with Ireland. And there were fewer trees.

Suddenly he got up and looked in the ash tray. It was empty. He walked quickly down the train after Owen and just saw him disappearing into the toilet. He knocked on the door but there was no answer.

'Owen. It's me. Owen.' He knocked again louder. 'Owen.' The bolt slid back to vacant and the door opened. Michael stepped inside and snibbed the door. Owen with the last of the man's bent cigarette-end between finger and thumb, cupping it in his hand, inhaled then flicked it into the toilet bowl.

'I'm mad at you, Owen. You know . . .'

'But, Brother . . .'

'Less of the Brother business. It's Dad. How can I let you smoke? What father would let his child smoke at the age of twelve? In public? Can you not wait for a fag until you get somewhere safe? Jesus, Owen, would you blow

45

the whole thing for the puff of a fag? You're extremely selfish.'

The boy stood mute and resentful, his underlip curled. He shrugged. Michael regretted saying what he had said. How could the boy help but be selfish? His selfishness was something he would have to learn to live with. Michael felt the fault was in him for applying his values to the boy. He had no right to.

'Hands above your head,' he said. He tapped his hands down the boy's pockets and took out a box of matches. 'Where did you nick those?'

'On the boat yesterday.' His answer was sullen. Michael felt another dozen lumps of sugar at least, but said nothing.

'You're not going to huff on me, are you?' He raised the boy's chin with his finger. 'So early?'

The boy gave a shrug, then smiled. He had good teeth.

'That's better,' said Michael. 'Let's get back.'

*   *   *

For hours the train charged through the countryside, through a landscape of fields, of slag-heaps and towns. Michael and Owen did not speak again, but sat opposite, their faces averted towards the window. The fat man came back, smelling of beer, and slept.

46

Michael wondered if he was taking the right line with Owen and his smoking. There would be no doubt in Brother Benedict's mind as to how to cure it. Six of the belt every time he smelt smoke on his breath. And a few times when he didn't smell it. That would put a stop to it. But Michael's reluctance to use the belt was one of the reasons why he had not got on with Benedict. He pictured the scene of himself strapping Owen for smoking in the john of a British Rail train half way across England. He had told the boy what it would do to his health, that it would eventually kill him, and if it didn't kill him it would drastically shorten his life, but Owen had shrugged. He said that he didn't care whether he died or not. Michael was taking on the task of giving him something to live for. His discipline of the boy must be positive, not negative like Brother Benedict's. Benedict had given himself away the day he had said sourly,

'Anybody who says he loves children doesn't understand them.'

He seemed to take a pleasure in using the belt. His little pre-execution phrases showed someone who was savouring the moment.

'Boy, I have been wanting to do this to you for a very long time,' or 'Long runs the fox' (a smile like a brittle flash of lightning), or 'Ponder these for the next hour or so, boy', and he'd bring the belt crashing down from a height, all his twelve wiry stone behind it. His

47

advice to Brother Sebastian had been to make it a deterrent,

'If it is going to be of any use to you, you must do it to really *hurt*. Otherwise you make a fool of yourself. Discipline, Brother Sebastian, is love disguised. The strap shows we care. It's the only thing they know. Kill and cure. Kill and cure. That's my motto. I was belted black and blue myself and what harm did it do me?'

Benedict seemed to enjoy his power over the boys, to make them do or say anything he wanted them to. One day, the previous winter, Benedict and Michael had been walking together. Snow had fallen and Michael was aware of the blackness of their soutanes and the fog of their breath as they strolled round the house.

'Wait till you hear this,' said Benedict. He called a boy who was passing. 'O'Halloran!'

'Yes, Brother.' O'Halloran came to attention.

'You know something about birds, don't you?'

'Yes, Brother, a bit.'

'Listen to the humility. Did you know of this expertise, Brother Sebastian?'

'No, I did not.'

'Well, Brother, O'Halloran here is our bird expert, our resident ornithologist. Am I not right, O'Halloran?'

'Yes, Brother.'

'They call him with a certain gentle irony

"the Bird Man of Alcatraz". O'Halloran, do you see those tracks there?' He pointed to the ground and the freshly fallen snow where some bird tracks had been imprinted.

'Yes, Brother.'

'Tell Brother Sebastian what they are.'

Michael leaned forward, interested in what the boy had to say.

'They're sparrow tracks, Brother.'

'Mmmmm.' Brother Benedict rubbed his chin. 'I'm not an expert in these matters, O'Halloran, but I would say ... mmmm ... they were eagle tracks.'

The boy stared at them. Michael watched.

'No, Brother, they couldn't be eagle tracks. They're too small and anyway...' The boy looked to Michael for help.

'Are you contradicting me, O'Halloran?' The voice was loud and rising in mock anger.

'No, Brother.'

'Good. Now tell Brother Sebastian what they are.'

'They are eagle tracks,' said the boy quietly.

'Very good, O'Halloran. Another lesson well learnt. Now off you go about your business.' Brother Benedict chuckled and rolled his eyes at Michael.

The incident left a bad taste in Michael's mouth although at the time he did not say anything. In later games like this Michael had seen boys turn insolent and Benedict would become genuinely angry and end by thrashing them. He was the only man in a mock battle who had live ammunition.

CHAPTER FIVE

When they arrived in London they sat in the huge station not knowing what to do, as people rushed in every direction as if certain where they were going.

'First things first,' said Michael. 'If we're going to stay in a hotel you can't go in looking like a Dublin jackeen. Let's walk for a bit and see if we can't get you a new rig-out.'

Owen carried the bag, putting his arms through the straps and hoisting it on to his back like a school bag. He leaned forward, an old man beneath his burden.

Eventually they found a large department store. Michael sat outside the changing cubicle while Owen tried on denim trousers and a jacket. Michael remembered the state of the boy's underwear and rushed off to buy him some. But he didn't know the size.

'What size of drawers for a boy of twelve?' he asked the girl behind the counter.

'Draus?'

'Yes, drawers. These.' He held up a pair of Y-fronts. She told him. He took two pairs and two vests and a few pairs of socks. The assistant offered him a wire basket and he piled the things into it. When he got back Owen was standing in front of a mirror, turning and admiring himself.

'The new man,' said Michael whistling. Owen seemed shy for the first time since Michael had known him, and coloured.

'Do they fit?' Owen nodded. 'Right let's have them.'

'We could nick them easy,' said Owen. 'Just walk out and leave the oul' ones there.'

'I've got money,' said Michael, a warning in his voice.

Michael bought him a pair of sensible shoes and a classy pair of training shoes, white with three blue stripes.

He thought that if the boy changed in the shop they might be stopped as shoplifters, even though he had the receipts. Attention of that sort was the last thing he wanted, so they found the nearest public toilet and Owen changed into his new gear. Michael felt nervous hanging about the toilet so he washed his hands slowly and thoroughly. He had heard things about London toilets and did not want Owen to be there on his own.

Owen came out of the cubicle carrying his old clothes in the new carrier bag. On the street outside they laughed and stuffed it into the black mouth of a waste bin.

'You look very grown up,' said Michael. Owen smiled and exaggerated his swagger so that it looked almost deformed.

'Are the shoes too tight?'

'No.'

'Then walk properly,' said Michael. 'Cowboys are out of fashion.' Owen laughed and punched him hard on the side. Michael put on an American accent.

'Man, I could use a beef-steak. What about you, son?'

'With chips?'

'Yeah, man. With chips.'

*   *   *

During the meal there was silence between them, apart from Michael interpreting the menu for the boy as best he could. It was something that Michael had not quite got used to yet, this silence. Owen seemed to control it, to clam up whenever he wanted to. It was as if talk was irksome to him and he would let it be known in a few grunted replies of 'I dunno' or 'I don't care'. Michael would then be quiet with him. He felt embarrassed when it was like this. The duty of keeping the conversation going rested entirely on him and when there was a void between them he thought it was his fault. He remembered the silences between his mother and father, warm full silences filled with the tick of the clock, but it was anything but that between Owen and himself. He blamed the age gap between them. He couldn't help but talk down to him. When there was

52

silence he wanted to manufacture something to say, no matter how silly it was.

But Owen could take the lead any time he wanted. When he was in the mood he could prattle on and on. He could joke and make up stories and talk drivel, mostly when they were alone or out of earshot of others. In silence he couldn't be shifted.

Round the corner from the restaurant they found what looked like a good hotel. Owen went round in the swing doors twice and Michael hissed a warning at him before going up to the reception desk.

'Could I have a room for the night, please?'

'I'm sorry, sir, we're fully booked.'

They got this answer at three more hotels and Michael was beginning to feel tired and angry when they finally got a place.

'A double room, sir?' asked the young receptionist.

'There's just the boy and myself,' said Michael.

'Would you sign here?' she said, pushing a black register across the counter to him and picking up her magazine. He panicked when she handed him the pen. Why hadn't he thought of it before? He should have had something prepared. Owen was taking giant steps from one unit of pattern in the plush carpet to another. He twitched the pen between his fingers. Smith was ludicrous. He stalled for time.

'What's the date?'

'The same as the entry above,' said the girl without looking up from her magazine. The title page of the story she was reading faced him. 'An Act of Love' by Garth Abrahams. He wrote in the register 'M. Abraham' and then after a moment's hesitation 'and son'. He gave the first Dublin address that came to his mind.

The girl showed them to their room and opened the door with a key attached to a large perspex tear-drop. Alone inside, they gazed at the room. It was beautifully furnished.

'All the colours match,' said Owen incredulously. He jumped on the bed nearest the window.

'Bagsy this one,' he said bouncing up and down. Then he stood up and trampolined.

There were two single beds with gold-coloured coverlets; the carpet and curtains were gold and similarly patterned; there was a desk and two Chippendale-type chairs upholstered in gold. Michael whistled and squatted, looking closely at the chairs. They had a bathroom off the bedroom, which Owen explored.

'Somebody's left their soap behind—and their towels,' he shouted out to Michael. Michael laughed.

'Idiot,' he said. 'C'mere.'

Owen appeared at the bathroom door. From his pocket Michael produced a packet of cigarettes and offered him one.

'If you want one now you can have it. But I still think you should stop.'

Owen took a cigarette and Michael struck the match and held the light for him. He smoked like a veteran, inhaling deeply. He lay down on the bed and watched the smoke drift up to the ceiling.

'All hotels leave soap and clean towels,' said Michael.

'Do they not always be nicked?'

'Everybody's not like you, Owen.'

Michael stood at the window, looking down at the grey roofs in the twilight. There were some remnants of red in the grey clouds. This had been their second full day together but it had all been spent travelling, and in a way did not count. A weariness came over him and all of a sudden he felt very tired. He hadn't realized the tension he had been under since they had left. Now that they were safe in a hotel under a different name he relaxed. He lay down on the bed and kicked his shoes off.

'It's bed-time for you, lad. You're bound to be knackered.'

'No I'm not.'

'We forgot to get you pyjamas, dammit.'

'Never use them outside the Home. I sleep in my vest.'

'Bully for you.'

Owen was going through the drawers in the desk and slamming them shut when he found them empty.

'Right enough, what are we going to do tonight?' he asked.

'We're going to bed. That's what. At least you are. At your age you need a full night's sleep . . .'

'But it's not even dark yet. At home I don't go till twelve.'

'You're not at home now,' said Michael, his voice quiet and threatening. 'If we're going to make this work, you're going to have to obey some rules.'

'Fuck the rules, Brother,' said Owen. He stubbed his cigarette out in the ash tray beside the bed.

'That's rule number one. There is no need for language like that. Rule number two is that you go to bed when I say. In an emergency the captain of the ship has the power of life and death over his crew. This is an emergency. I am the captain. I say beddybyes. Do I make myself clear?'

Grudgingly Owen stripped off. As he was getting into bed, Michael looked over at him.

'Jesus, look at the feet,' he said. 'How long is it since you had a bath? Don't get into those sheets like that. Do you mean to tell me you put new clothes on over that lot? Let me see.'

Michael inspected his feet, which were black with ingrained dirt at the heels and between the toes. He looked him all over. There was a watermark of dirt about his collar bone and the back of his neck was filthy.

'Into the bath,' said Michael. 'How long is it since you had one?'

'I don't swim every day like the rest of them. Anyway, the water won't be hot.'

'In hotels the water is always hot. This is not the Home.'

The boy was offended and Michael was sorry he had spoken so harshly. He knew from experience that the one thing that hurt the boys was to be called dirty or to be accused of having a walking head. They could take pride in worn and dirty denims just so long as they themselves were not seen to be dirty.

Michael ran the bath for him, making sure it was not too hot. Naked, the boy looked fragile, his shoulder blades jutting like wings, his ankles, elbows and wrists nodules of bone. Across the back of his legs, as if in a continuous line, was the shining skin of his scars. His body seemed blue-white, not flesh-coloured, a plucked fowl colour.

'If you turned sideways you'd disappear,' laughed Michael.

Prudishly the boy sheltered himself by bending over and holding his elbows. He ran for the bathroom. His bum like two pale eggs disappeared round the corner. Michael yodelled, 'TAAAARRRZZZAAAAAN.'

While Owen bathed, Michael unpacked. He listened to the boy's voice imitating an engine and the gurgle and swish of the water. The sound of a diving plane was interrupted by a yawn, then continued to rise in pitch. Michael lifted the clothes that Owen had strewn about the floor and folded them. His trousers and new jacket he hung in the wardrobe. As he closed the door the metal coat-hangers clashed softly together in the emptiness like the slow tolling of thin bells.

CHAPTER SIX

He had met Owen for the first time about three years ago. He had just finished a lesson when word came through from Brother Benedict that he was wanted in his office. He hung his apron in the cupboard, brushed the sawdust from his soutane with the palm of his hand and walked to the Superior's office. Reception was the only part of the place which had carpet. The hypocrisy of it annoyed Michael every time he walked on it. Outside Brother Benedict's door there was a small traffic light divided into three sections: Enter—Engaged—Wait. Michael knocked and after a long moment heard Brother Benedict call 'Come in' in his posh voice. Benedict was behind his desk, looking over his half-glasses; to the right was a woman slanted sideways in an armchair; to the left, standing by a wooden upright chair, was a small boy. A Guard, his hands behind his back, was leaning against the

58

bookcase.

'Brother Sebastian,' said Benedict, 'this is Mrs Kane and this . . .' he waved his hand slightly in the boy's direction, 'is her son, Owen. In the special circumstances of the boy's age the powers-that-be have thought it best that Mrs Kane be here at his inception, as it were. You may sit, Brother Sebastian.'

Michael took the hard chair beside the boy. The woman was too heavily made up. She gave the impression of having put make-up on her face without washing it first. Her mouth was small and red and pinched, pulled tight as if by purse strings. She looked old enough to be Owen's grandmother. Her hair was dull and combed for the day.

'Mrs Kane has been filling us in on some background information on Owen.' The woman nodded, drumming her nicotined fingers. 'And I have been assuring her that the boys who arrive here thimbleriggers and termagants are the least of our worries. But we do not send them out that way. Do we, Brother?'

Michael nodded agreement.

'Kill and cure is my method, Mrs Kane. You can rest assured that if anything can be done to put this young man on the right path then it is we who will do it. There may be pain in the process, Mrs Kane, but I'm sure that we have your backing—and for that matter, the State's.'

Mrs Kane nodded vigorously, snapped open

her handbag and pulled out a packet of cigarettes. She tentatively offered the packet in the direction of Brother Benedict. He refused with the palms of his hands and his face slightly averted.

'No thank you, Mrs Kane.'

'Is it all right if I . . .'

'Feel free.'

Mrs Kane lit a cigarette with a small bronze lighter, pulling hard on it with her tight mouth and taking it between her knuckled fingers. She crossed her legs and Michael noticed that her thighs were scuffed with psoriasis, blotches of crusty skin, obvious through her tights.

'You've no idea what a trial that boy has been to me,' she said. 'He was my last hope—after the way the others have gone. I've done everything for him and this is the thanks I get. I let him get away with far too much. If I'd been like some mothers I know t'would have been a different story. He has me nearly driven mad. I can't take it any more . . .'

Her mouth puckered and she began to cry silently, the tears brimming over on to her cheeks.

'Don't worry yourself, Mrs Kane. He's not worth it,' said Brother Benedict. He turned to the boy. 'You see what you have done, boy? Reduced your mother to tears.'

'It's not the first time either,' said Mrs Kane snuffling into a used ball of a lilac tissue she produced from the bottom of her bag.

'I hope you're proud of yourself,' went on Brother Benedict. 'Your mother has sacrificed herself for you totally. She has struggled to rear you and you repay her by starting your life as a criminal. Do not worry, Mrs Kane, we will return you a different boy. The guttersnipe you bring us will not be the boy you get back. Brother Sebastian, will you show Master Kane to his quarters?'

Throughout the boy had been standing with his hands behind his back, looking down at his toes. He seemed glad to be walking out of the door. In the corridor his shoulders drooped with relief and his hands slipped into his pockets. Michael warned him about the hands in the pockets.

Later, when Michael went back to the office, Brother Benedict was doing half twirls in his office chair, smoking. He tapped the ash off his cigarette and said,

'What a revolting woman. A despicable piece of goods.'

Michael turned to go out. Brother Benedict called after him,

'Oh, I should warn you—the boy takes fits.'

'Fits?'

'Yes, Brother Sebastian, fits. Epilepsy. You know?'

The worst and most damaging attack that Owen had had was in the gym one January day. Everyone had gathered to watch the Home play a posh grammar school at basketball. Brother Benedict and all the staff sat in a nook on the sidelines, protected behind a table. The boys were lined along the tops of the wall-bars. Everyone had been warned beforehand that there was to be no barracking of the visiting school. Brother Benedict made it seem almost an act of charity for them to come and play at the Home. The boys, in their turn, should treat them, if not with politeness because they had not got that in them, then at least with respect. The school had turned out in a smart strip—green vests with the school emblem on the chest, green satin shorts and green socks. The Home had unironed regulation white. The sniggers, raised eyebrows and limp-wrist gestures of the boys on the wall-bars were soon stopped when the grammar school began to play. They quickly went 25–3 in the lead. The umpire's whistle shrilled; then it happened in the silence of the first time-out.

Owen, who had been one of the boys perched on the wall-bars, let out a screech and toppled down behind them. There was a gap of about a foot between the bars and the brick wall. Owen slithered down, but because of the wall-bars, remained upright during his attack. He gyrated and threshed, his knees and legs unable to bend. His head pummelled on the bars. His eyes rolled and he made strange noises. Brother Sebastian ran from behind the table, clambered up the wall-bars, the skirts of his soutane flying, but could not reach down to the boy.

'The pipes. He's getting burnt by the pipes,' someone yelled. Owen continued to jump and twitch like a puppet behind the bars. His hair was too short for Brother Sebastian to get a grip on it and he himself was too bulky to squeeze his shoulders down to reach his clothing. The grammar school boys stood staring. One of them nervously began pounding the ball off the maple floor in a static dribble. And still Owen's attack continued. There was blood on his face and collar now and he was making a noise in his throat like the draining of a sink. Brother Sebastian jumped down and reached his hand through the wall-bars. He bunched up the front of his jacket into a fist, then raised the struggling boy a little. He put his other hand through a higher wall-bar and raised him a little more, still gripping his clothes. Slowly he inched him up behind the bars. Other boys—the older ones—saw what he was doing and came to help, slipping their hands between the bars and easing the stricken Owen to the surface.

Brother Benedict stood at the table, his fingers splayed and his face white. Later he said to Michael, 'Although I'm an educated man, it is easy to see how, in the past, it was construed as demonic possession.'

For weeks afterwards Brother Sebastian's forearms were mottled and blue with bruises.

Owen would bear the scars of burns from the pipes for the rest of his life.

* * *

Michael lay in the darkness, watching the streak of yellow light from the crack in the curtains swing from one side of the ceiling to the other. The London traffic seemed to go on until all hours. The sound of Owen's breathing came quick and regular from the other bed.

Michael opened his eyes and knew that he had no chance of going to sleep. He had been keeping his eyes tightly shut and his jaw clenched. He tried to relax but could only do so when he was conscious of it. Each time his mind returned to the past his jaw tightened up and he found his fists were knotted. A drink might help him sleep. He dismissed the thought, not wanting to leave the boy on his own so soon. What if he should wake up? Or even worse. He looked at the green specks of his watch and was amazed to see that it was only a quarter to eleven. He got up and dressed quietly in the dark and went downstairs. Little harm could come to the boy sleeping.

The same girl was still sitting at reception, looking more bored than ever. She was painting her nails with blue nail varnish which had flecks of silver in it. She directed him to the bar, calling him Mr Abraham after a quick glance at the open register in front of her.

Michael, after the quiet of trying to sleep and the silence of the foyer, walked into a room rowdy with noise. The bar was crowded, the talk almost drowning the background of piped music. He ordered himself a pint.

'Bitter?' said the barmaid and he nodded. What a strange thing to call a drink. Bitter. Aloes. Sorrow. For something that was supposed to make you feel happy. Vinegar on a sponge offered as an act of kindness. One of the Brothers had told him of being in Rome and drinking a wine called 'Tears of Christ'.

He sat down in a free corner with his pint. He didn't want to talk to anyone and hoped that nobody, drunk or otherwise, would disturb him. He always found it difficult to lie. He was no good at it—although he thought he had done not too badly in the past two days. Normally he found himself speaking the truth even though he didn't want to. Once on holiday with another Brother, both of them in civvies, they met two nice-looking girls who laughed a lot. They were getting along fine until his asked him what he did and without a moment's hesitation he said he was in the Brothers. He didn't want to say it but it had just come out. After that the other Brother spent the rest of his holiday hitch-hiking on his own.

Michael knew that he must get himself into the frame of mind where lying came naturally to him. His and Owen's future depended on it. If it was left to Owen, there would be no difficulty. They would have to work out a story which both of them knew and stick to it no matter what situation they ran into. In the Home Owen's lying had been professional, but Michael felt he had got inside that. He felt that the boy told him the truth now, although about some things he was not absolutely sure. Things he could not verify about his mother, about his past.

Owen had told him that his mother had tried to kill him. Michael found difficulty in believing this story. Was the boy just looking for sympathy or was it horribly true? Some of the details seemed genuine—but that was the mark of a professional liar, to get the details right.

Owen said that his mother had been drinking all night—vodka with orange juice. She had had a man with her and she had made Owen go to bed early. Sometimes when this happened he sneaked out of the window on to the flat roof and climbed down the pipe, then through the back yard into the street. The back-yard door had been torn off its hinges many years ago and never replaced. This night he stayed in bed and listened to the voices and silences between the man and his mother, until he fell asleep.

It must have been the slamming of the door as the man left that wakened him. He lay awake waiting for his mother to come to bed. He heard her open the bedroom door and he closed his eyes and pretended to be asleep. He heard her stagger against the plywood wall. She was mumbling to herself. He felt her ease the pillow out from under his head and he thought she was going to take it for herself. Then suddenly he felt it close over his face. He began to struggle and shout but she pinioned him tight where he lay. He remembered wondering if it was another kind of fit that he hadn't had before and he was imagining it all, with the breathlessness the only real thing about it. He screamed and gasped and managed to turn his head sideways where there was air. He felt her hand try to force his face back into the pillow and he bit it, as hard as he could. She screamed and for a minute let go of him. He wriggled away and ran for the light of the other room. He heard her call after him drunkenly,

'If it wasn't for you . . . ya wee shit!'

Those were the words she had used, he said. He then went on to tell what happened when a neighbour found him in the bottom hallway behind the bins wearing only his vest. Owen had spun him a few lies and had been taken in to his downstairs flat for the night. The man had provided him with striped pyjama bottoms with white draw cords, big as a tent, and had helped him roll the legs up until they reached Owen's ankles. The next morning the boy went back up to his own flat. His mother had cried most of the day and had given him the money for enough chewing gum to last the week.

When Michael asked him about the story later, on different occasions, it remained substantially the same. There were some differences. Once he said that his mother had brought a cushion from the other room. Another time he said it was the man *upstairs* who had found him. Michael did not like to trip him up by grilling him on these points, for, on a matter so serious, it would have displayed a terrible lack of faith.

His bitter had inched its way down the glass without him being aware. He bought himself another. The crowd had become very noisy, laughing and shouting to make themselves heard above the din. There was no one drunk like in Ireland, but looking around it was hardly an English pub. The people in the bar seemed to be mostly tourists and foreigners. He had heard American accents and the girls in the opposite corner looked Spanish, like the posters of dancers. He felt secure in this atmosphere. If they mixed with the tourist crowd they would be very difficult to trace. Just another holidaymaker and his son.

The beer had begun to relax him and he felt warm. He actually felt he was on holiday. There was plenty of hope that they could make it. He yawned, finished his pint and felt that he could sleep.

On his way upstairs he noticed that the receptionist had finally gone. In the bedroom he put the light switch down slowly, minimizing the snap as it went on. He went over and looked at Owen as he undressed. He was still breathing normally. His elbow was high on the pillow over his head and his face was turned into its crook. The bedclothes had been pushed down about his waist and his new vest had rumpled up. His rib-cage, each bone outlined, rose and fell. His eyelashes were long and dark. Suddenly the boy smiled, not a grin, but a deep warm satisfied smile. Then he snuffled and began to snore lightly.

Michael had not seen that look on his face before. It depressed him, the thought that the only way the boy could be really content and happy was when he was sleeping.

CHAPTER SEVEN

The next morning at breakfast Owen made the waiter smile by asking for a third plate of cornflakes.

'Leave room for something else,' said Michael. But he needn't have bothered. Owen then went on to eat sausages, bacon, fried tomatoes and to finish what toast and marmalade was on the table.

'It'll not take long to fatten you up at this

rate,' said Michael.

'Smashin',' was all Owen would say.

'What we need is a map of London. Then we can plan what to do.' Owen shrugged. In the foyer Michael bought an *A-Z* of London and they took it to their room to study it. From their window, Michael could see that it was a bright sunny day.

'Right,' he said. 'Let's not waste too much time over this or the best of the day will be over.'

Michael suggested various places he thought Owen might like to see, the Tower of London, the Zoo, Buckingham Palace, the Houses of Parliament, but the boy just shrugged and said 'I dunno' after each one.

'Is there anything you want to see?'

Owen thought, screwing up his eyes. Then his face became animated. His eyes widened and lit up.

'Any slot machines?' he shouted.

Michael sunk his head in his hands.

'Aw God, Owen. The capital of the world and all you can think of is slot machines. Where do you think you are, Bundoran? There's no slot machines in London.'

The boy sat on the unmade bed and swung his feet.

'Anywhere you like then,' he said.

'I think...' said Michael. He paused. 'I think ... we're not organized. There's confusion in the camp. I think...' He began again. 'We'll go to Piccadilly and start from there.' He stubbed the Underground map decisively with his finger. The boy looked at the maze of coloured lines.

'There's a couple of things we *have* to do today,' said Michael, clapping his hands together.

'What?'

'Get our story right, for one. And buy a radio.'

'Smashin',' said Owen.

*   *   *

Michael did not like to admit it to the boy, but he was stunned by the Underground. The moving stairs that bore them down to the guts of the city, the stopping each time they came to a sign to interpret it as people rushed around them. Northbound or southbound? The speed at which the trains thundered into the stations, pushing a warm gale in front of them. He kept assuring the boy that he knew what he was doing. On the platforms Owen stood very close to him. After only one mistake they arrived at Piccadilly.

Above on the pavement, Owen let out a shout:

'Look. Look, Brother!' The boy was dancing up and down, pointing. He stuck out his tongue at Michael. Michael followed the line of his finger and saw a huge amusement

71

arcade, its double doors open, its machines whirring and whining, their coloured lights flickering.

'Can we go in?'

'O.K.,' Michael laughed, 'but we're not going to spend all day.'

But they spent the best part of an hour and about four pounds as Owen ran from one fruit machine to another. Michael stayed on the same machine, thinking it was bound to pay out sooner or later. His only substantial win was on three lemons. They also played T.V. games in various forms, trying to shoot one another down as British and German pilots, condemning one another to horrible deaths in knocked-out sunken submarines.

Eventually Michael could stick the noise no longer. The air was full of the whine of diving planes and gunfire and police sirens and clattering coins. A policeman had been standing inside the door for some time and Michael kept an eye on him. He seemed to be scrutinizing the crowd, which was mostly teenage lads.

'Come on, Owen. Let's go.'

'Just another while.'

'No.'

Michael took him firmly by the shoulder and led him towards the door. The policeman gave them a funny look as they left.

They began to walk round Piccadilly. The sun was shining and it was warm. In the crowd

Michael felt relaxed. He was about to say something to Owen when he discovered he was not there. He spun round, his eyes searching for the boy's blue denim and blond hair. He began to retrace his steps, slowly trying to batten down the feeling of panic that was rising inside him. The crowd surged about him in both directions. Faces he didn't know or want to know. Then he saw him. Standing by a shop window full of magazines. Girls pouting forward clutching their breasts, with their legs open, bums, flesh. He grabbed the boy by the shoulder and shouted,

'OWEN, DON'T WANDER AWAY FROM ME.'

'Would you look at that,' said the boy, not taking the slightest notice of Michael's anger. Michael pulled him away, the boy still looking over his shoulder at the window.

'I can just see it now,' said Michael. '"Yes, Officer, I want to report a missing boy. I know he couldn't find his way back to the hotel. So he's well and truly lost—in London, a city of . . . fourteen million? Yes, you see we ran away together from a Borstal in Ireland. No, I'm not his father." That would be just great now, wouldn't it? All because you want to look at women's . . . things.'

The boy curled his lip.

'Knock it off,' he said.

'You stick by me, you hear?'

They wandered down Regent Street until they came to a toy shop. The boy was excited looking in the window, pointing out things to Michael. He was jumping from one window to another.

'Let's go in,' said Michael.

It was the biggest toy shop they had ever seen. Owen climbed on a rocking horse but got off when Michael told him it was only for young kids. He rushed up the stairs, hardly daring to think what would be on the next floor.

When they had seen it all Michael said that the boy could pick a couple of things. He suggested, thinking ahead to the days when it would be wet and they would be stuck in their hotel room, that he get something to make. He pointed out some glider kits. The boy chose the biggest one.

'I'll help you make it,' said Michael. He pulled a bundle of notes from his pocket and peeled off two fivers. 'And enough glue to stick it together,' he said to the assistant. He also bought him a gun, a realistic matt black Lüger, and a throwing knife.

The next big department store they came to they went in and bought a radio.

'Will it lift Radio Eireann?' Michael asked the assistant.

'Pardon?'

'Can you get the Irish programmes on it?'

'On the medium wave you should be able to.' She fiddled about with the controls, changed the position of the radio. Through a

74

faint hiss Michael heard the familiar voice of Gay Byrne.

'Yes, that's it,' he said. 'Don't move it from there.'

He paid for the radio and the two of them walked through the store to the street.

In another shop he bought a small cash book and some reading books for Owen to practise on.

They came to Marble Arch and saw the green of Hyde Park behind it. They decided to get some hamburgers and Coke and eat in the park because it was such a nice day. They collapsed footsore on the grass among their parcels.

After a while Owen said, 'Play a game of knifie?' Michael got slowly to his feet. He had not wanted to buy the knife but he put it down to being a matter of trust. He must trust the boy.

'Stand with your feet together,' ordered Owen. They took turns at throwing the knife and sticking it in the ground a few inches from their feet. Each time they had to put their feet on the spot where the knife had stuck until eventually they were both doing the splits.

'Remember Finbar Waters?'

'Will I ever forget?'

Waters was a boy who, just over a year ago, had attacked Michael with a bread-knife in the dining hall. He was a boy on the verge of madness. He had thrown a potato at the boy opposite and when Michael had spoken to him he had screamed, run to the top table and grabbed a bread-knife. He kept screaming 'Sebastian Bastard' over and over again as he tried to stab him. But Michael had the strength of him. He nearly broke his arm to get the knife off him. Afterwards Waters was sent to an asylum.

Brother Benedict's only comment on the affair was, 'Waters—the universal image of affliction in the Bible. Thus—he is in it up to his neck.'

Michael asked the time and Owen told him it was one twenty-eight. Only two minutes to wait for the Radio Eireann News. He switched on and turned the volume up as loud as it would go. Owen pulled the rings of the Coke cans. The radio was angled for the least interference. The news came on.

In Northern Ireland a girl of five had been shot dead in crossfire, but there was nothing about them.

'Might we be on the news?'

Michael nodded. The boy was delighted with this idea.

'Why do you think I bought the radio?'

In any case he was glad of it because it eased the silence between them as they ate. After a while ceilidh music came on and they both lay down, Michael his face to the sun, the boy on his belly.

Michael couldn't help feeling slightly

annoyed at the boy, annoyed that Owen had not once thanked him for any of the presents that he had bought—the watch, nothing. He argued with himself that the boy had never been *taught* to thank people, that he had rarely, if ever, been given presents before. Nevertheless he felt irked that the boy had not the spontaneous goodwill to say thanks.

The ceilidh music drummed on at his ear. The tunes all seemed to be the same.

'Is there no good music on that thing?' said Owen, as if echoing Michael's thought.

'Hold it,' said Michael, getting up into a sitting position. He took a piece of still tacky Sellotape from the wrapping round one of the parcels and stuck it on to the perspex waveband of the radio to coincide with the pointer at Radio Eireann.

'Now we'll never get lost,' he said and twiddled the knob until he heard sounds of rock music.

'That's better,' said Owen.

Michael gathered up the litter they had created and stuffed it into a bag. He was on his knees and pretending to jive to the music.

'Hey, Michael.'

'What?' It was the first time Owen had used his real name.

'Here's something for you.'

The boy extended his hand to Michael. In it was a cardboard and cellophane pack. It was a Papermate pen. He broke open the cellophane

77

and took it out.

'It's a beauty. Thanks.' The boy grinned. Michael's voice suddenly dropped a tone. 'Where did you get it? You have no money.'

'In the shop. Where you bought the cash book.'

'But you have no money.'

The boy shrugged and smiled.

'You can wipe that smile off your face,' shouted Michael. 'Do you realize the risk you took? Jesus, Owen, if you're caught at that game and hauled into the manager's office it's the police. COPS. They'll be swarming all over us asking questions and THAT'S IT. Prison for me and an express trip back to the Home for you.'

Michael shook his head in disbelief and shuddered at what had nearly happened to them. When he looked back at the boy he saw he was crying. It was the first time he had ever seen him cry. Not even after the beatings in the Home, or the time his collar bone was broken had he seen tears come out of his eyes. He fiddled with the pen, not knowing what to do. The boy came towards him and Michael put his arms around him, He was still kneeling and the boy came to the height of his head. He encircled him with his arms and hugged him. He felt Owen relax into his hug and cry more bitterly, shuddering with each breath.

'O.K., Mister,' Michael said. 'It's the nicest present I ever got. But why didn't you nick a

78

better one?'

The boy laugh-cried into his shoulder. Michael groped for a hanky and gave it to him. He noticed a park keeper walking in their direction. He held the boy at arm's length.

'Dry up and let's go,' he said. Owen stopped crying and turned to watch the uniformed keeper walk past them.

'Never again?' asked Michael.

'Never again,' said Owen. 'Your chin is rough.'

*   *   *

In the hotel before tea, listening to the Radio Eireann News, Michael heard that a man was wanted by the Gardai to help them with their enquiries into the disappearance of a twelve-year-old boy, Owen Kane. The Gardai, said the newscaster, were treating it as a case of kidnapping.

CHAPTER EIGHT

That night they were so tired with the walking they had done that they sat in the lounge and watched television. There was something wrong with the set and the people looked squashed and dwarfish. When they turned sideways they had green haloes down their spines. Michael suggested that they go to their room and begin building the plane. Owen shrugged, more in agreement than anything else.

Because of their lack of preparation it was some time before they got started. They had nothing to cut the light balsa wood, so Michael devised a tool from his shaving kit. A razor blade with one edge rendered safe with a double layer of sticking plaster. Owen laid out the kit on the desk but still they could not get started. Michael wanted to get something to stop them cutting through and ruining the desk top.

The girl at reception was removing the blue and silver speckled nail polish she had put on the night before. She raised one pencilled eyebrow when Michael asked her for the loan of a bread board from the kitchen, and the other when he asked for a ruler.

When Michael arrived back with the bread board and ruler Owen was sitting vacantly stroking his cheek with a small sheet of balsa wood.

'It's like a feather, not like wood. Here, feel,' and he stroked the white light wood across Michael's cheek.

'I can't feel it with three days' growth.'

'Are you growing a beard?'

'I think I might,' he said, kneading the stubble of his chin. 'It might be safer.'

Owen let the balsa sheet fall and it

zigzagged to the floor soundlessly. He stared at it fixedly against the gold of the carpet.

'Come on. Snap out of it. I'll help you with the plans.'

Being with the boy continuously, he noticed these little trances more and more. After a moment's staring silence the boy would do a double-take.

'What?'

'Let's get to work.'

They pored over the unfolded sheet of instructions and Michael set Owen various things to do. He did not want to make the glider himself and yet he felt that if he didn't give him a guiding hand the boy would make a mess of it.

'Can you read what it says?' asked Michael.

'Yes.'

'Liar,' said Michael and began to read the words and point to the diagrams. The exploded view simplified things. The boy began to measure and cut. A slight pressure on the blade and it just sank through the wood with a creaking sound, leaving a clean cut. The delicate skeleton of one of the wings began to build up. The glue left wisps, cobwebs hanging from it and stuck to their fingers. Every so often it had to be pulled away like a second skin.

Owen was good with his hands, working neatly and with precision. Michael began the second wing. They became absorbed in their work so that Michael noticed neither the silence between them nor the time. It was almost one o'clock when they decided to go to bed. The two wings, almost completed, stood propped in a V on the desk as if plummeting.

The room was saturated with the tangy smell of glue and they slept heavily that night and through the morning until almost lunchtime.

*   *   *

After what was a mixture of lunch and breakfast they sat alone in the chintz-covered armchairs in the lounge. The chairs were old-fashioned, with high sides which came up to Owen's shoulders. He sat looking boxed in, with just the tips of his toes touching the ground.

In the next room a children's party had started. The guests had been arriving throughout lunchtime in their tweedy coats and good clothes. Cars had pulled up outside and left them off. There were both boys and girls, and each one carried a parcel. The game that was being played now was noisy. The music, a pop record turned up to full volume, drummed so that they could hear the bass notes and the rhythm from where they sat. Every so often it would stop in the middle of the tune and be followed by a second's silence. Then they heard squeals and cries and laughter.

'Would you like to go in?' he said to Owen. The boy nodded a slow definite no.

'I could ask whoever is running it.'

'I'd hate it.'

Again the music stopped, the stunned silence, the screaming.

'Come on, I'm going to make you go in. All those nice wee girls? Come on, you'll love it.'

He took the boy by the arm and Owen began to fight him. He struggled and kicked and punched.

'I don't wanna go,' he shouted. Michael saw that there were tears of embarrassment in his eyes and he stopped and laughed.

'I'm only kidding,' he said. He lifted one of the cushions and threw it hard at him. It hit the boy softly in the face.

'Big get,' said the boy, the words muffled in the cushion. Michael knew he was offended. He tried to win him round.

'Right, young Kane. What are we going to do today?'

He didn't answer. He just lay in the chair, his knees drawn up to his chest and his head in the cushion.

'Owen? What do you think? Eh?'

The boy said something inaudible into the cushion.

'What was that?'

He lifted his head. He was smiling.

'Go to the amusements.'

'No, not again.'

'The toy shop?'

'We want to go *new* places. See *new* things.'

'*You* do.'

'I am the captain of this ship,' said Michael in his captain's voice, 'and what I say ...'

'I want a smoke,' said Owen. They went up to their room and Owen smoked a cigarette. Then they went out to wherever Michael wanted to go.

*　　　*　　　*

This time Michael, with his *A-Z* in hand, walked away from Piccadilly. The day was good but just not so warm and bright as the previous one. They came to Leicester Square and Owen noticed a crowd of people at the side of the pavement. He tugged at Michael's sleeve and pointed. They moved over to see what was happening. A loud fairground voice was coming out from the middle of the crowd. Owen wormed his way in, pulling Michael after him. A man in a navy raincoat was standing in front of an upturned orange box, flicking cards about its surface. He kept up a constant patter:

'Find the lady, find the lady. The simplest game in the world. Make yo'self a few quid. Just find the lady. I'll show 'er to ya just to make it easy.'

He showed the Queen of Hearts and two black Jacks, then flipped them down on top of the box.

'Which one is it? Which one is it, ladies and gents? Put your money where your mouf is.'

A man leaned forward with a five pound note and tapped a card. The man in the navy raincoat turned it and it was the Queen.

'Right, he's got it. The gentleman wins himself a fiver,' and he paid out for all to see.

Owen tugged at Michael.

'It's dead easy. I can see which one it is. Get the money.'

A man with a heavy moustache, standing beside Michael, spoke: 'It's easy, mate. It's the one in the middle.'

The man who had won before won another fiver, picking the middle card.

'Get the money out,' hissed Owen.

'Yeah, go on,' said the man with the moustache.

Michael put his hand in his pocket and pulled out a roll of fivers. He was going to peel one off when the man who was turning the cards turned to talk to someone. The man with the moustache leaned forward and bent the corner of the Queen, marking it.

'Now you can put the lot on,' he said in a whisper.

The dealer turned round again and shouted,

'Find the lady, the simplest game in the world.'

He flipped the cards, leapfrogging them over each other. Owen hissed,

'Now. Put the lot on.'

The one to the left had a crimped corner. Michael hesitated, still about to take off one fiver. Suddenly the man with the moustache snatched the money out of his hand and plonked it down on the card on the left. The dealer flipped it over. The Jack of Clubs. He grabbed the money. Michael spun round but the man with the moustache had gone. By the time he turned back the dealer had the cards and the money in his pocket and he was throwing the orange box in the doorway. He strode away and was joined by the man who had won the first two fivers and the man with the black moustache. The three of them disappeared round a corner before Michael could even think of following them. The small crowd of people dispersed. Michael ran to the opening the men had gone into. The street was full of shoppers going to and fro.

'Jesus,' he said between his teeth.

'Get the cops,' said Owen, who had caught up with him.

'All your brains must be in your bum.'

They stood saying nothing for a long time, parting the crowds that moved along the street.

'How much was it?' asked Owen.

'I don't know. There must have been sixty there.'

'Bastards. We've no luck,' said Owen.

'Luck,' mocked Michael. He was seething with anger. He had gone pale. 'I hate being taken. The stupid Irishman. Come on.'

They walked and came to Trafalgar Square. They sat on a bench for about an hour without a single word passing between them. People were buying small tubs of grain to feed the pigeons and having photographs taken as the birds landed on arms and heads. Again and again Michael felt surges of embarrassment at having been so foolish as to take his money out in a crowd. He was also aware that Owen was feeling sorry for him and that made it worse.

'Thimbleriggers,' said Michael at last managing a smile. 'That's what they were. Thimbleriggers.'

'Benny,' said the boy in disgust.

'One day I tried to find out what it was. The dictionary says it's people with cups. A ball is under one cup and they swivel them about. Crooks. It's just the same trick with cards.'

'I hate him, the big shite,' said the boy.

'It's sleight of hand . . .'

They lapsed into silence again. The boy had reason to be bitter. Michael remembered one incident that stood out more than the others. He had been teaching Owen's class first thing in the morning. It was a cold morning and their breath was visible even inside the large woodwork room. Brother Benedict sent for Owen and the boy returned after about half an hour, his face white and his teeth clenched against crying. He held his hands tight beneath his armpits. The rest of the class shouted,

'Brother, look at his wrists.'

Michael paid no attention but later asked Owen to stay behind. He looked at his hands and wrists. They were swollen and red. On the wrists were several horse-shoe-shaped welts, crescents where the blood had been brought to the surface, but the skin had not broken.

'How many did he give you?'

'Six.'

'It's a cold morning for it,' said Michael. 'What was it all about?'

When he heard the story the whole thing seemed ludicrous. Someone had stolen a can of spray paint from the technical block and written in huge awkward letters: BENNY DIES O.K. Brother Benedict thought it was Owen.

'What made him think it was you?'

'He said they were my initials.'

'What were?'

'O.K. means Owen Kane.'

'Holy Jesus,' said Michael. He half walked, half ran to Brother Benedict's office and ignoring the 'engaged' sign by the door, went straight in. Despite the sign Brother Benedict was alone. He swung round in his chair and looked over his glasses.

'Ah, Brother Sebastian. I was expecting you.'

Michael began, the words becoming slurred in his haste to get them out before his courage failed him.

'Brother Benedict, I must protest in the strongest possible terms about the ... the

88

thrashing you have just given Owen Kane.'

'And why is that?'

'He did *not* sign his name to *any* slogan.'

'Brother Sebastian, I'll thank you to calm yourself.'

'Did you say that the boy signed his initials to some graffiti?'

'I did.'

'O.K. is a slogan itself. They just add it to things.'

Brother Benedict took off his glasses, folded the legs flat and rubbed into the corners of his eyes with finger and thumb.

'Brother Sebastian, do you think I'm a fool? Credit me with a little more intelligence.'

Michael did not know how to react. He was confused.

'You know and I know,' said Brother Benedict, 'that we could never find the real culprit. By now the boys know that punishment has been meted out. Someone has got it in the neck. It may deter others from doing the like again, for fear their mates get it. The O.K. is just a little irony of mine. "Benny dies O.K." Now the boys know that Benny has risen.' He bunched his big fist and swung it in a slow punch, clicking his tongue at the supposed moment of impact.

'K.O.,' he said with satisfaction.

For the next week Owen had to try and clean the slogan off with a pad of steel wool. To reach it he had to stand on a stool.

'It's sleight of hand,' said Michael again. 'The quickness of the hand deceives the eye.'

'That's not how they did it,' said Owen. 'They just robbed you.'

'True.'

*   *   *

The next morning Michael heard on their transistor that the search for the missing boy was being moved to London. Certain people had come forward with valuable information. He said smugly that London was a big place.

At breakfast Owen was quieter than usual. He didn't say a word.

'What's wrong?' Michael asked. The boy did not answer, clinking and scooping at the remaining milk in his cornflake dish.

Later he said,

'I don't like this hotel. Let's move.'

'Why?'

The boy shrugged.

In their room Owen sat on the bed.

'There *is* something wrong. What is it?'

Owen looked over his shoulder and nodded at the bed.

'What?'

He pulled back the sheets. The bed was soaking wet and acrid with urine.

'I see,' said Michael.

'Let's leave. Right now,' said the boy. 'We'll never see them again. Nobody'll know us.'

Michael thought for a while.

'O.K. If it makes you feel happier.'

Recently that had become the reason for all his actions.

CHAPTER NINE

Their next hotel was not as good as the first. When Michael had given in to Owen he had asked for his bill to be made up right away, because they were leaving. He packed everything into his bag except the wings and pieces of the glider which were scattered over the desk. These Owen carried by hand, gently and delicately between finger and thumb, down to the taxi. He went back to the room for two plastic carrier bags of toys.

In the taxi he sat surrounded. Michael sat on the small seat with his back to the driver, holding on to the strap. Going round corners, Owen reached out both his hands and rested them gently on the flimsy bits of wing and fuselage, steadying them.

Michael decided to change his name again, and this time had the foresight to have thought of one before he went into the hotel. He leaned forward to Owen and said in a whisper that it was worse than being married. Buying a ring and changing names.

'And having a child,' said Owen and they

both laughed. The name he chose was O'Leary and he announced it loudly to the clerk as Owen stood behind him, plastic bags propped at his feet, holding bits of the pale balsa skeleton.

The furniture in the hotel was tatty and, as Owen pointed out, did not match. The headboards of the beds were scratched and the bedside table had several long cigarette burns on it. Other pieces of furniture just seemed to have been left in the room. A wardrobe, a dressing table, some upright chairs with sagging seats and an old bookshelf filled with dog-eared books. The only hint of luxury was a black telephone beside one of the beds.

'Anyway it'll be cheaper,' said Michael. Owen wanted a cigarette and he let him have one. He lay on the bed, his head resting on his hands, smoking like a lord. Suddenly there was a knock at the door and Michael saw the cigarette retract into the cup of Owen's hand like a snail's horn.

'Give it to me,' said Michael, and he held it between his fingers. It felt light and unusual and he didn't know how to act with it.

'Come in,' he shouted.

'Sorry, Mr O'Leary. Here's your fresh towels.' She was a small woman with a flowered cross-over apron. Her voice was Irish. She left the towels over the end of the bed and told them that the bathroom was just at the end of the corridor. She hesitated, standing

92

with her hands crossed.

'Thank you very much,' said Michael.

'Ah, you are Irish,' said the woman with an even stronger brogue, now that she knew she was among friends. 'When Mrs Finlay said there was a Mr O'Leary in Number Ten needing towels, I said to myself he's sure to be Irish. What part are you from? No, wait a minute. Say something and let me guess.'

Michael put on his best Dublin accent. He felt foolish and shy as if speaking into a tape recorder.

'My name is Michael O'Leary and this is my son, Owen. Owen O'Leary.'

'Eh well, now. Dublin I would say without a doubt. Am I right?'

'Near enough,' said Michael hesitating.

'And isn't he the lovely boy,' she said, putting her head on one side and looking at Owen. The ash was growing on Michael's cigarette and he didn't know what to do with it. He looked round for an ash tray but couldn't see one.

'And what age are you, Owen?' said the little woman.

'Twelve.'

'A man almost. But right enough, Mr O'Leary, what part are you from?'

'Swords.' He didn't know why he said Swords. It was the first place that came to mind.

'Swords? SWORDS d'ye tell me? Sure I

have a sister living in Swords.'

The ash fell on the carpet. Michael changed the position of the cigarette to his other hand, half raised it to his mouth, but thought better of it. He had no luck of any kind. People took his money from him, Owen wet the bed, and now the first place he can think of, she has a sister living there. With a sinking feeling he realized what the next question would be.

'Whereabouts in Swords d'ye live?'

Michael changed the cigarette from hand to hand again. There was more white ash on it.

'Do you smoke much, Mr O'Leary?'

'No, not much. On holiday,' he smiled.

''Tis bad for you and bad example for the boy,' she began to scold.

'Is there an ash tray about? Do you see one there, Owen?'

'Wait. Hold on. There should be one . . .' and she fussed about the room looking until she found one on the window sill. It was an inverted lid of a Maxwell House coffee jar, black and stained. She held it while Michael stubbed the cigarette out.

'There's nothing but God's clean air should go in the lungs, Mr O'Leary. Am I right? Anyhow I'll let you get on with it. But sure I'll see you before you go, please God. How long'll you be staying?'

'Just a couple of days,' said Michael.

'Gooday then to both of ye. Enjoy yourselves,' and she was away.

Owen was rolling about the bed laughing. Michael joined in nervously.

'D'ye smoke much?' mimicked Owen.

'Nosey oul' bitch,' said Michael.

'Is she the owner?'

'Naw, she's some sort of cleaning woman— or a hotel detective.'

*　　　*　　　*

The next day it rained, heavy rain that ran in shudders along the street. In their room Owen stood looking out of the window, his elbows resting on the sill. Michael lay on the bed reading the *Daily Express*.

'Did you take your Epilim yet?' Michael asked.

'No.'

Michael lifted the bottle and rattled it. 'You know what'll happen if you forget.'

The boy took a tablet with a mouthful of water, crouching at the tap of the wash basin.

Michael scratched his five-day-old beard. The hair of his head was black but already he could see orange and ginger streaks appearing on his chin. He didn't like the thought of a piebald beard and wondered whether he should shave. It itched annoyingly. He asked Owen.

'Naw. It looks good. Makes you look like a baddie.'

'A baddie?'

'Yeah, like a baddie in a cowboy film.' He shot Michael several times from behind the cover of the dressing table with pinging ricochet sounds. With a groan Michael rolled off the bed and was dead before he hit the floor. Not quite dead because he had just enough breath left to raise himself up and gasp,

'You done me wrong . . .' and then fall truly dead.

Owen grinned from behind the outcrop of rock, then walked slowly across to where the body lay. He turned it callously with his toe. The body's tongue was protruding grotesquely and his mouth was all slanted. The eyes bulged white and the pupils rolled back into the head.

'Yo'r dirt, man, jest dirt.'

Michael said, 'Quit the clowning,' and got up to look at the books on the shelf. Owen still wanted to play and began slow motion punches at the small of Michael's back, saying 'wham' and 'splatt'.

'Cut it out,' said Michael. 'It's time you were doing some work.'

'What kind of work?'

'School work. That's what.'

'Aw come on, Mick.'

The books on the shelf looked as if they'd been left by guests over the years, or bought at a jumble sale to fill a shelf. There were some detective stories, a gardening book, romantic novels, two handbooks for different makes of cars, and a clutter of other stuff. Michael pulled out a Ladybird reader and flung it on the bed.

'Let me hear you reading that,' he said. Owen opened the book and began,

'"Peter is here. Jane is here and Pat is here. Here they are. Here they are in the water. They like the water."' Owen began to make fun of it, reading in a singsong voice '"Pat likes the water. Pat likes FUN. Come in Pat. It IS fun. It is fun in the wat-ter. Come in the wat-ter. Come, come, KUM."'

'O.K.,' said Michael. 'Cut it out. So you're a genius.'

'It's crap,' said Owen.

'All right, Mister Smart-ass. Let's find something a bit harder. Except for the Home you weren't at school long enough to know the teacher's name.'

'Miss McGuckin.'

'Let me see . . .' he said scanning the books on the shelf. 'Ah, a children's book. It says "For young people".'

The book was *The Age of the Fable* by Thomas Bulfinch, an Everyman copy with a faded brown cover. He looked at a page and saw how difficult it was.

'Have a go at that, Smart-ass.'

Owen opened the book.

'What's that word?' he said, pointing.

'Daedalus,' said Michael. Owen began to read haltingly.

'"Daedalus built the . . ." what's that word?'

'Labyrinth.'

'"Daedalus built the labyrinth for King Minos, but afterwards lost the—favour—of the King and was shut up in a—tower. He con-con-contrived to make his—escape from his prison, but could not leave the iz land by sea . . ."'

'Island.'

'". . . As the King kept watch on all the ves-ves—" what's that?'

'Vessels,' said Michael without looking.

'How did you know? You couldn't see.'

'It couldn't have been anything else, could it? Vests?'

Owen read with painful slowness down the page.

'". . . so he set to work to make wings for himself and his young son Icarus. He rouched feathers together, the larger . . ."'

'He what?'

'He rouched.'

Michael looked over his shoulder and laughed.

'Wrought,' he said. 'It means to work.'

'". . . and the smaller ones with wax and gave the . . ."'

He stammered to a halt. Michael took the book off him and began to read it aloud.

'"Icarus the boy stood and looked on. When at last the work was done the most skilful artificer, waving his wings, found himself buoyed upward and suspended on the beaten air. He next equipped his son in the same manner and taught him how to fly. He said, 'Icarus, my son, I charge you to keep at a moderate height, for if you fly too low the damp will clog your wings, and if too high the heat will melt them. Keep near me and you will be safe.' As he said these words the face of the father was wet with tears and his hands trembled. He kissed the boy, not knowing it was for the last time. Then he flew off, encouraging him to follow. As they flew a ploughman stopped his work to gaze, and a shepherd leaned on his staff and watched them, astonished at the sight and thinking they were gods who could thus cleave the air.

'"The boy began to soar upward as if to reach heaven. The nearness of the blazing sun softened the wax which held the feathers together and they came off. He fluttered with his arms, but no feathers remained to hold the air and as his mouth uttered cries to his father it was submerged in the blue waters of the sea."'

Michael stopped reading. He set the book quietly on the bed between them and they were both silent. The rain gusted and rattled at the window. Michael sat with his head in his hands. The playful mood of a moment ago had disappeared completely and they sat, each knowing the other was depressed. The hotel plumbing sang in the pipes as someone used the bathroom at the end of the corridor.

'This has happened before,' said Owen.

'What? Déjà-vu?'

Owen nodded. 'Yes, the story of the boy falling into the sea, the noise of the pipes, you sitting with your head in your hands.'

Michael got up, concerned.

'You'd better lie down. You're not going to have an attack are you?'

'No. If it doesn't happen right away it doesn't come.'

'Are you sure? Lie down anyway.'

The boy lay on the bed. He looked paler than usual and Michael was worried.

'Do you want me to read some more?'

'Naw, it's crap.'

Michael lay down on the bed beside him and put his arm round his shoulder.

'You say that about everything. Like it or not, you're going to have to be able to read and write. You're an intelligent lad who never went to school.'

'I did so.'

'Aye, about as many times as I went to dances. Do you feel O.K. now?'

'Yes.'

'What do you want to be? Still a footballer?'

Owen nodded and Michael felt the nod in the crook of his arm. He said,

'And you don't have to be able to read for that.'

'Is it still the Arsenal?'

'Yes.'

'How'd you like to go to a game?'

'A match?'

'Yes. Highbury isn't too far from here. We'll go on Saturday.'

The boy's eyes were wide with astonishment. It seemed to Michael that the boy had never associated Arsenal with reality. The wall above his bed had been covered with cut-out pictures of the team, red and white against the hospital green. He had drawn a crudely lettered sign for 'The Gunners' in red felt-tip pen. The idea that he could actually go and see them in the flesh seemed to amaze him.

'Maybe they'll give you a trial,' said Michael.

'I'm too young for a ...' Then he saw Michael laughing and he began to punch him as he lay on the bed. He stopped.

'Will all the Irish players be on? Liam Brady?'

'I'm sure. If he can make the first team.'

Owen in his excitement ignored the taunt at his favourite player.

'And Jennings? And Pat Rice?'

It was as if the team he was to see on Saturday couldn't possibly be the same team he had adored for years. There would be some cheat in the end. For Owen there always was.

CHAPTER TEN

When Michael told him that Arsenal were playing *away* the next day, Owen shrugged and his face said, 'I might have known.' Michael promised him that if they were still around, Arsenal were playing Manchester City the next week and they could go to that.

The days passed quickly, each day in itself long and full, yet when it was over it seemed barely to have happened. Having got over their curiosity about the Underground, and having got lost several more times, they began to take black taxis everywhere. It was expensive but it had the advantage of not being a journey to nowhere.

They went to all the places that the tourist guide recommended, Madame Tussaud's, St Paul's, the Tower, sailed up the Thames and spent two hours, which was two hours too many for Owen, in the British Museum. They came out footsore and weary.

One day they went to the Zoo. Birds in cages turned glittering yellow eyes on them as they passed. Owen was wary of them, remembering the seagull. The smaller birds all seemed regimented, standing in rows making electric noises, continuously sharpening their beaks on the branches where they perched. When they came to the Aquarium, Owen liked it immediately. Tanks of slow languid fish trailing lengthy skirts of tail and vivid lightning shoals which could disappear in an instant and reappear just as quickly with a change in direction. Unlike the birds in their cages, they seemed free, in their element, and gave no sense of doing laps around their tank. Each swim was a new journey.

A uniformed attendant clicked his way down the hall, his hands behind his back.

'Hey, Mister, have you any flying fish?' Owen asked.

'No, sonny.' He walked on a little, stopped and came back. 'I believe,' he said, as if he knew all about it, bending forward from the waist, 'that they are difficult to keep. Bang themselves offa the glass all the time. Kill 'emselves, they do.' He winked at Michael over the boy's shoulder and said, 'It's a better question than the one about fish fingers,' and clicked his way up the hall, leaving Owen staring after him.

'Smart cunt,' said Owen.

The boy agreed to most of these trips provided that they could go back eventually to Piccadilly and have an hour on the slot machines. He never came out winning but when he was there Michael could see the delight and excitement on his face. Michael too, although pretending reluctance, enjoyed it when he had to join in some of the games, table football, T.V. tennis, shooting. He never consciously let the boy beat him and, once he had agreed, he took part as if it was a real competition. Owen always beat him at football. The plastic doll players, somersaulting in unison, always seemed to be in the wrong place at the wrong time for Michael, and the ball would slam into his goal.

Owen loved too to play the pinball machines. Michael watched him pull back the spring-loaded piston and send the steel ball racing among the glittering obstacles, springing back and forth to the clink of bells and flashing lights and the buzzing and clicking of the counter as the score mounted to incredible thousands. And yet every game, no matter how nimbly the boy operated the small rubbers which batted the ball back for another score, Michael knew that eventually the ball would trundle out, rattling hollowly in the dark guts of the machine and the score would return to zero. That was luck—his luck. He knew it and knowing it did not reduce his disappointment every time it happened.

Once they went back to the big toy shop in Regent Street and saw a machine for stamping T-shirts with a photograph. Owen said he wanted one with Michael's picture on it. Michael stood smiling into the camera with his ten-day-old beard bristling and a look of disbelief on his face. Then Michael said he wanted one with Owen on it. The machine clattered and typed across the plain surface of the two shirts and came out the other side with their photographs on. That night they wore them to dinner in the hotel and for once the waitress smiled.

The conversation between them grew, the boy contributing more, Michael feeling more relaxed in the inevitable silences. They laughed a lot, the boy's childish sense of humour not being so far from Michael's own.

One of the best laughs they had was the morning Owen woke up, having wet the bed. Michael was loath to move hotels yet again and after a thinking breakfast they went back to their room. Michael went out into the corridor with Owen at his elbow. He knocked on the door opposite but got no reply. He tried the door but it was locked.

'Damn,' he said. He moved down the corridor, knocking quietly on doors and when there was no response trying the handle. Then he found one open. He tiptoed in and called,

'Anyone at home?' There was no reply. 'Quick,' he said to Owen and they rushed back to their room and stripped the soaking sheet off the bed. It had elasticated sides. Michael bundled it up and they ran on tiptoe back down the corridor laughing.

'It stinks,' he said. They quickly pulled back the clothes from the other bed and stripped the sheet off.

'You keep an eye out,' hissed Michael. Owen went to the door with a suppressed wheezy laugh. Michael lifted each corner of the mattress and inserted it into the shape of the wet sheet. Then he made the bed quickly over the top of it. He lifted the dry sheet and ran.

Back in their own room they laughed at the thought of some Lady Muck sleeping in the bed.

'Oh, Rodney, this bed's ever-so-damp,' said Owen. He was useless at an English accent and this made it even funnier.

'Kane the Stain strikes again,' said Michael. He turned over Owen's mattress, stained with a dark jagged outline, and put on the dry sheet.

'You're a crafty bugger, Sebastian.'

'Just don't piss the bed every night, that's all,' and they rolled about laughing on the newly made bed.

In public places, where they could be overheard, Owen called him Dad and gradually Michael began to accept this, not as a game but as reality, and because he was beginning to accept the father role as real he made other attempts to teach the boy some lessons, but they ended in frustration and angry words.

Towards the end of the week Michael began to notice the speed with which his money was dwindling. On Friday night, after Owen was asleep, his unease about the situation forced him to count it. He was shocked to find how little he had left.

*　　*　　*

He could not sleep. Long after he had snapped the cash book shut and dropped it on the floor beside the bed, he lay with his eyes open. He heard voices on the street below and got out of bed. He opened the curtains and looked down but could see no one. The yellow sodium lights made haloes in the rain droplets on the window. Occasionally a car engine changed its note as it came to the hill on which the hotel was built. Somewhere not far away he heard a factory churning through the night. Michael had never liked the city—any city—but he knew the mentality of country people well enough to know they would be conspicuous in a village. The city hid them and he was grateful and annoyed at the same time.

He had been raised in the country, on a small Ulster farm outside Ballycastle. The place had been poor, although they had never gone really hungry.

A grey cement house, surrounded by a clutter of out-buildings set with its back to a hill. In the middle of the buildings and at the back door of the house was the yard, always in his memory glistening with muck. The front door, which had a small concrete path on to the road, was rarely, if ever, used. The only times he could remember seeing it open were at his parents' funerals. When his mother died, and as she lay stiff and white on the bed, his father with rusted garden shears wept as he cut the front door free of the overgrown rambling rose so that her coffin could be taken out that way and not through the mucky yard. The front door had been closed originally to preserve the beautiful rug in the front hallway. Then with habit the passageway had fallen out of use and Michael, at his father's funeral a fortnight ago, had seen the rug in the dark behind the closed door, still covered with its sheet of clear plastic.

There was a rule that wellingtons had to be left at the back door, and his father padded about the house in grey socks. Always the heel of his sock worked its way to the arch of his foot after a day in the wellingtons. His mother knitted the socks when she was well enough.

When he was five she had been crushed against a concrete gatepost by an unruly heifer. The doctor said that she would be paralysed from the waist down for the rest of her life.

'It's the spine,' his father had said, and had a bed set up for her downstairs. She lived on like this for six years, knitting when she was able, crying when she was not. Each night before the family rosary, his father would freshen her up, washing her face and hands with a damp face-cloth. Although she could do this herself, she always let her husband do it. It became a sort of ritual, when he would caress her face with the cloth, looking at it as if for the slightest speck of dust. Then she would put her head down and let her hair fall forward while he washed and massaged her neck. She always said that part was nice.

'Michael, give me my beads out from under the pillow,' and they would kneel at her bedside by the slight ridge of her legs beneath the coverlet and recite the rosary.

His father did everything for her. Michael felt that he sacrificed his life for her. He refused to have a nurse in and, with the time taken up looking after her, the farm began to go down.

He was a man who had respect for every living thing. Although he was plagued by rabbits, when the myxomatosis came he would take the trouble to kill them with a blow of his hand as they sat trembling, saying that he did not want to waste a cartridge on them. He pulled chickens' necks so fast and expertly that they never felt a thing. He showed Michael the best black pools, with their slow wheels of foam, to find trout and taught him how to distinguish the various birds of prey. The sparrow-hawk, the kestrel, the harrier, and when they were on Tor Head, the eagle. If he saw a hawk he would stop and freeze and watch until it was out of sight. He would put his hand on Michael's shoulder and whisper, 'Watch now, son, and you might learn something.' They would stand and watch the bird hovering in the air, as his father said, 'like a trout facing upstream', and watch it stoop out of sight, or if they were lucky see the kill. The fact that he lost several lambs a year to them did not diminish his admiration for them. 'The rulers of the air,' he would mutter, almost in disbelief. And yet he hated the gulls. In early May he took the boy on climbing trips around the cliffs and rocky coves to smash the eggs of black-backs. Dropped, they broke on the rocks far below with a moist click.

'They're a curse,' said his father. 'They do more damage than enough. They'll peck the eyes out a lamb before the ewe can get her born—aye, and the tongue too. They'll leave it in such a state that there's nothing left to do but kill it.'

He was a perfect father, yet Michael was sure that never once had he thought of his role as a father. It came so naturally to him to communicate his enthusiasms, his warmth. When he was with his father he felt safe. Nothing could touch him. His grip of iron as he helped his son across rocks. Wearing full-length waders he could still lift Michael bodily across white water.

'Stiff elbows,' he would say and Michael would hold his elbows stiff and tight by his sides and feel himself hoisted into the air by his father's cupped hands. This was the way they had got into football matches. In the rush at the turnstiles Michael's father would swing him up with the warning, 'Mind your head,' then pay for himself and push through after his son.

'Two for the price of one,' he would chuckle

on the terrace.

He had once taken Michael to an All-Ireland Semi-final at Croke Park. For Michael, the yellow jerseys of Antrim, the crowds, the excitement—everything was ruined by the return journey on the train.

Everyone except his father seemed to be drunk. Michael was put in a window seat and his father half shielded him from the crowds passing up and down. They couldn't get a seat in a compartment but had to make do with the open carriage. At the station, before they even left, there had been a fight and the Guards had led a man away with snot and blood coming from his nose. The men on the train wore yellow and white paper hats and rosettes. They staggered and fell as they tried to walk the train. People were singing and shouting and women were screaming. Once Michael had to go to the toilet and his father walked close behind him, a large hand on each shoulder. The place, when they got there, was covered in sick. The aisles of the train were black and wet with spilled bottles. They rattled about as the train swayed. His father, all the time, seemed terribly angry and kept looking at his watch. When they got back from the toilet he said,

'Try and get some sleep, son.'

He covered him with his coat but Michael could not sleep. His eyes darted with nervousness, watching the procession of staggering men. Then two men started to fight

111

just opposite them.

'Then you're no fuckin' Irishman,' screamed one of them. He had a bottle in his hand and smashed it against the metal edge of the seat, leaving a dagger of brown glass in his hand. Michael's father leapt to his feet and walked over to them. Michael flung off the coat but still sat huddled on the seat. The one with the bottle turned on his father and made an upper cut at him with the broken bottle. His father stopped the blow and twisted the man's wrist behind his back.

'A fine example of Irish manhood you are,' he said. He made the man drop the bottle. He talked closely into his ear. Finally he let go of him and the man turned and put his arms around him.

'No offence, nofence meant. Nofence, nofence, pal.' The man was crying. Michael's father guided him out of the carriage and looked at his watch once again. He was white around the mouth.

'Try to get some sleep, son.'

But Michael couldn't. Even now as he twisted on the bed sleep would not come to him.

One day he remembered well when his father had taken him in to Ballycastle to fish from the pier. His father crouched, a small blackened tin box at his feet, sorting through the hooks with a careful finger. He had just lost another hook in the thick leathery

112

seaweed to the left. It had been a bad morning's fishing—one small mackerel and three lost hooks. His father selected a hook and squeezed the fat worm on to it. He cast it far out to the right but before or just as it hit the water, a gull swooped and snapped up the bait. His father stood in amazement, the rod still in his hand and the gut whining off the reel.

'Lord God,' he said. He snapped on the brake and braced himself for the tension. The gull was pulled round in a wide arc above their heads.

'I can't leave it in that state,' said his father and began to reel the bird in. It made the most awful squawking, like the shearing of metal. It jinked and twisted and changed direction so that his father had to keep turning on the pier to keep from getting his line tangled. A crowd had gathered to watch. Some people were laughing. He brought the bird down in a flurry of grey and white. Michael was amazed at the size of it and its large yellow beak open like a pair of scissors with the fishing line disappearing into it. His father struck it hard on the back of the head with a piece of wood and it cowped forward, its wings outspread, like a broken W. He struck it again and again until it was dead. Then he snipped the line and dropped the bird over the side of the pier. He looked up at Michael, and smiled.

'It's a bad day when the biggest thing you

113

catch is a seagull.'

Michael wondered why it was the tragic things that remained with him most vividly. The cat that had been killed by a lorry at lunchtime in front of his house. That day they had tapioca for lunch.

This was the summer that the Brothers had come recruiting to the school. Michael was due to leave at the end of the year and, full of piety and enthusiasm, put his name on their list. At first his father had not fully approved, hoping that Michael would stay to take over the farm. But he accepted with good grace, saying the decision was up to the boy himself.

Michael wanted to be to Owen what his father had been to him. He looked round now at the boy as he slept. His mouth was open and his hair tousled. He wondered if this is how he would feel about a child of his own. If his child would have the love and trust to fall asleep in the presence of someone else. He bent over and kissed him on the forehead and knew that the boy would not have permitted it if he had been awake.

As he stood over the bed, his mouth still puckered from the kiss and the boy muttering and turning, Michael was conscious of the time he wasted. He was aware of the times when he was unaware. Tracts of the day when he did not heed what the boy was saying or doing. It was lost time, never to be regained. The same set of circumstances could never be repeated.

If asked, he would undoubtedly say that he loved the boy, but there were many times when it didn't seem like it. Michael knew that their time together could end at any minute and to waste any of it was a regret to him. Not to probe, to respond, to teach actively was to throw away an opportunity. Michael lay down on his own bed, his hands cupped behind his head. It had been like this with the Brothers. He knew now that his time there had been wasted. His life had been governed by a series of prohibitions and, while God existed for him, this was acceptable. But once he ceased to believe in the God of the Brothers, all he was left with was a handful of negatives. His vow of poverty did not worry him much because it was a condition he had been used to most of his life on the farm, but those of chastity and obedience did.

The Novice Master had constantly played the humility card, speaking as he always did, with his face averted from his audience.

'Pride, Brothers, is one of the worst sins of all. I see Lucifer on useless wings plummeting into the sea of Hell for all eternity because of it. It is only by subjugating your will to the will of others—and God—that you will find your true self. If you want to find strength, give in to others without a murmur. When you have whittled away everything that makes you who you are, then that is your true self.'

Michael found nothing at the end of the

process of self-whittling. He had no true self. He told this to the Novice Master, who looked out the window. It was some time before he answered Michael.

'You have not yet gone far enough. There is a hard core in you that resists you giving up your will. You must continue to try. It may take a long time but you must never give up.'

Eventually Michael fell asleep with his jaw taut and his fists clenched.

CHAPTER ELEVEN

They were walled in by people and Michael had to lift Owen so that he could get a glimpse of the pitch.

'Stiff elbows,' he said and the boy held his arms bent and stiff against his sides. Michael hoisted him above the heads.

'Can you see?'

'Yes,' shouted the boy. Michael felt him quiver with excitement.

'Time?'

'Two fifty-six.'

'This is useless here. Let's get down the front,' said Michael.

They threaded and elbowed and pushed their way through the crowd until they came to a crush barrier not far from the front. Owen followed in the passage that Michael created, holding tightly on to the back of his anorak. Michael, acting a bit simple, indicated the boy and got himself a place at the crush barrier. He lifted Owen on to the bar so that he could see, and held him there with his arms round him.

He was stunned by the new season green of the pitch, its flatness and the precision with which it was marked in white lines. At home he had played on fields tilted to the side of a mountain or with a hillock in the middle hiding the goal at the far end, the whole area measled with pats of cow dung. He had forgotten that at this level of the game everything could be so perfect.

The teams came out and Owen cheered himself hoarse when he saw the red and white strip of Arsenal. He recognized the players from their photographs and pointed them out, screaming and laughing at the top of his voice to Michael. In pale blue, the colour of a blackbird's egg, Manchester City were kicking into the goal nearest them. They were knocking about what looked like five brand new footballs. Owen looked over his shoulder and shouted,

'It's smashin'.'

'It hasn't even started yet,' roared Michael. The crowd chanted and sang incessantly and deafeningly, holding up red and white scarves and banners.

It was then that Michael noticed the crowd to his right. They were in their late teens. Most

117

of them had their heads shaved so closely that their hair was only a shadow. They wore blue denim waistcoats with no shirts so that their arms and chests were bare. They were shouting at the field as if in intense and uncontrolled anger. Oathing and making obscene gestures. One of them openly pissed into a beer can, splashing those around him, and hurled it into the crowd. They all had their scarves tied to their wrists. Owen watched them.

'I'd like to see Brother Ben belt some of those bastards.'

'He'd have a job,' agreed Michael.

The group was pushing and shoving to clear a space for themselves and those around them were standing back, pretending not to notice them. Michael watched them out of the corner of his eye as the game started. He knew that Owen was doing the same, the way he was twisting on the bar. Then the boy turned and said,

'I think we could see better from down there.'

Michael agreed with him and they moved away from the group, down nearer the field.

'A bit to the left in case that gang throws anything more,' said Michael. This time it was Owen who led, squirming his way into the wall. He got a place and Michael stood behind him, his hands on his shoulders.

Then suddenly the boy went stiff. Michael felt the change in him beneath his hands, the rigidity. He leaned down to be on a level with his face. He shouted into his face.

'Are you all right?'

The boy was staring forward, his eyes wide, his jaw dropping slowly open.

'Oh Jesus, Owen, not here.'

The boy's body began to jerk and his head flicked back as if his neck was broken. His arms threshed and trembled, but the press of the crowd held him up. A young lad next to him elbowed him shouting,

''Ere, whatcha doin', mate?'

Still the boy was jerking and threshing, his eyes rolled back up into his head so that only the whites showed. Michael pinioned his arms and as best he could crushed the boy up against the wall to stop him kicking.

'Help me, will you? He's having a fit,' screamed Michael. Above the noise of the crowd Michael could hear the sickening noise in Owen's throat. His fear was that he would swallow his tongue or bite it off.

'Get a doctor,' yelled Michael.

'No chance, mate.' The young lad had become concerned, seeing the colour of Owen's face, like blue wax. 'Get'm on to the park.' The lad helped Michael heave Owen into the air. Other hands came to steady the boy's twitching body. He fell on the other side of the parapet wall and, for a terrible instant, looked to Michael like a fish as he arched and flapped on the track.

119

'Oh Jesus,' he cried into himself. 'Help him. Help him.'

The lad made joined hands for Michael to step up and climb the wall. Owen's fish-gawping mouth was open and there was foam and spit around it. Michael sat on his legs and searched his pockets for something to put between his gnashing teeth. He found a pencil but could not get the teeth open. He was afraid of being bitten, of losing his fingers. The boy snapped again and he got the pencil in. He was making a high-pitched whine now. The pencil shattered between his teeth. Michael got most of it out, lead and painted wood, snatching at it. A lollipop stick lay by Owen's head, and fumbling and praying and cursing, Michael wrapped his handkerchief around it and inserted it between the boy's teeth. The arms were still quivering and waving. It was as if thousands of volts were being passed through his body. A line of faces on a level with the track watched, stunned. The crowd swayed and roared and chanted at the game.

To Michael it seemed like hours before anyone came to help him. An ambulance man came running, clutching his bag to his side, and knelt down beside them. He quickly bound the boy's ankles together and his arms to his sides. Another ambulance man followed with a stretcher.

'I'm his father,' shouted Michael into the ambulance man's ear. He walked with them

120

round the pitch to the tunnel, his eyes fixed on the blue-white face of the boy bobbing on the stretcher. His hand was poised over the stretcher, keeping him from falling off when his back arched and he squirmed from side to side.

As he walked he frantically tried to remember the name he had used in the hotel. There would be doctors, statements, maybe even hospital. There would be policemen. At the first hotel he had used Abraham, but over the second name he had a mental block. He must remember it. Would they phone the hotel to check? Once the police heard his accent, would it spark something off about a man and a missing boy?

Then from nowhere the name came. O'Leary. That was it. He felt calmer. In the sick room beneath the main stand Michael and the ambulance men sat and watched the fit subside. Gradually the boy quietened, the intensity went out of his movements until eventually he lay still. Above them they could hear the crowd, muted like the rising and falling of the sea. The boy opened his eyes and he looked around, confused as to why he should be lying in this place.

'It's O.K. Lie still. You've had an attack,' said Michael. He began untying the bandages at his sides. The ambulance men received another call. They were left alone in the room together.

'How do you feel?' Michael asked.

'O.K.,' said Owen.

'Do you think you could walk?'

The boy nodded and tried to get to his feet. Michael steadied him with his hand.

'I think we'd better get out of here before they start asking a lot of questions. Can you walk?'

'Yeah. Can we go back up to the game?'

'We're going straight back to the hotel and you're going to your bed. Don't be so stupid, Owney.'

In the corridor on the way out there was a small riot. Two policemen were dragging a youth who was shouting and struggling. One of the policemen had a hatchet in his hand and the youth's face was covered in blood. He was screaming like a woman. Michael and Owen pressed themselves up against the wall to let them pass.

'How the hell do we get out of here?' asked Michael. Two more policemen stood outside a room, their arms folded. Michael went up to one of them.

'The boy here has been very sick,' he said. He put his arm round his shoulders. 'How can we get out of here?'

The policeman was sympathetic and led them through corridors to the exit.

'It's like a maze,' said Michael. He thanked the policeman and they found a taxi easily because the game was still only in its first half.

When they got back to the hotel Michael undressed the boy. He stood limp and tired, almost unaware of what was happening. Between the sheets he fell into a deep peaceful sleep. Michael sat on his own bed looking at him. During the fit the boy had become someone else, animal-like almost. The image of the fish was the one that stood out in his mind. Flapping and vibrating in the dust of a pier. He knew from experience that the boy would sleep like this for many hours. He could be left without Michael having to worry about him.

In the Home there had been a medical orderly who had looked after Owen when he had had a fit, but now Michael had the sole responsibility. He needed to find out more about the disease, but he could not risk going to a doctor. He remembered a bookshop several streets away and decided to go along and see if he could find anything.

Being Saturday afternoon, the street was crowded. He looked at the faces as they jostled past him. He found himself in the strange position of wanting to see someone he knew. For days the fear had been with him of bumping into an acquaintance from home, but now it no longer existed. He searched the faces knowing he would see no one—millions of them, bespectacled, balding, sullen, worn, all of them faintly resembling people he had once met, so that he was always on the verge of a greeting or a nod. If he had seen someone, he had no doubt that he would have ducked away, but he could not rid himself of the longing. He wondered if this was homesickness.

In the bookshop Michael did not know where to begin to look. He had never been a great reader. He found a small medical section but could see nothing on epilepsy. In another section he saw an encyclopaedia and looked it up under E. The book was heavy and he laid it on a bench and read the article through, but it didn't tell him much that he didn't already know, describing epilepsy in terms of an electrical brainstorm. One thing that he hadn't known made him smile because it was such a coincidence. He read, 'A typical symptom associated with epilepsy is the fugue. The sufferer may leave home, travel for several days or weeks without seeming to have full realization of what he is doing. Although not fully conscious, he is able to abide by the rules of society, e.g. respecting traffic regulations.' He closed the book and muttered, 'The fugue, how are you?'

CHAPTER TWELVE

The waitress remarked on the boy's absence and Michael explained to her that he had been sick and was now sleeping. He arranged for some food to be sent up to Owen when he awoke.

Eating by himself he found an odd experience. He missed the boy sitting opposite him. Even though they only said one or two words to each other during a meal, he missed that too. He ate looking around him, conscious of the irritating squeak and scrape of his knife and fork on the matt pottery plate. The rain had come on and was gusting against the large picture window looking on to the garden. Outside the trees threshed and single summer leaves spiralled into the air.

What disturbed him most about eating on his own was the way his mind kept running away with him. Mentally he kept pulling on the reins and saying Whoa! every time he thought about what they were going to do. His mind shied away from the fence of the future. Their money was steadily draining away. What happened when it finished? Could he get a job somewhere as a joiner? Buy a flat, settle down with the boy, call him his son? The possibility of adoption frightened him, not because of its commitment, but because they would be bound to be found out.

He wished he had bought a paper to occupy him. He read the menu over once again.

Fresh garden peas. His mind relaxed into the past again. Brother Benedict had put him in charge of the kitchen garden at the Home and he had loved every minute of it. Preparing the ground with sweat, the feel of the hard dried peas as he dropped them into the trench, some of them shaped like green cubes, the spears of them bursting through into the air, the weeding and training upward on dead twigs and finally the eating. Cracking open the hollow pods and letting six fat peas run down his hand into his mouth as he stood waist-high among the rows. If the joinery didn't work out he could get a job in market gardening, maybe. Owen could go to school. He liked the idea of the comprehensive schools here. But again, would there be any papers needed? Interviews, lies. 'What school was he at before?' A lie. 'We'll write off then for some details. What's the address?' Forget it. He was back on the same track again.

He looked around the room. A man was wiping his mouth with a paper napkin but there was ice-cream on his lapel. A woman with winged glasses sat alone chewing furiously and politely, her lips pulled tight, her cheeks bulging.

The brassicas. He had liked the brassicas the best. The most difficult to grow but they had the highest rewards. Their big, purple and blue veined leaves, the yellow-white florets of the cauliflower, cracking the leaves over to keep the heads white. Watering the cabbages, leathery, the water remaining in single droplets, glittering and rattling with a hollow sound. Diamonds. Like diamonds, the way it remained in the nooks and crannies of the leaves afterwards. It was Owen's word. He had made the comparison one day when he had helped him with the watering. Michael had always found him so willing. If only he could be like that with other people, with strangers. His stubbornness and lack of respect for others would get them into trouble. In a school he would be in trouble within a week and the headmaster would . . .

Michael banged down his coffee cup too loudly and some people turned to look at him. He left the dining room and went quickly up the stairs to look in again on Owen. He hoped the boy would be awake, but when he opened the door he heard his deep even breathing.

He took a book off the shelf and stretched out on his own bed. He tried to concentrate but found himself reading the first paragraph again and again. The sound of the wind buffeting the window and booming in the chimney distracted him. Small rattles of soot fell behind the hardboard of the blocked-off fireplace. He threw the book away and turned on the transistor very low. He placed it by his ear on the bedside table. It was nice background music, swinging from one tune to another without any warning.

Michael must have fallen asleep because when he opened his eyes it was getting dark.

He immediately looked over at Owen's bed. He switched on the bedside lamp and the boy stirred. He opened his eyes and ran his bitten fingernails through his hair in a mock scratch.

'Hiya,' he said.

'How do you feel?'

'O.K. Bit weak.'

Michael helped him up in the bed and made a back for him out of two pillows. He had often done this for his mother, folding one pillow double and slanting the other against it. The boy lay back limply. His face looked washed and clean.

'Where's the music?' he asked. Michael indicated the transistor.

'Boy, were you in some state today.'

'Was I bad?'

'It's as bad as I've seen you. The only thing was you didn't wet yourself this time.'

'Thank God.'

'You don't remember any of it?'

'Naw,' said the boy. 'The only bit I can remember is just before. Just before it starts.'

'I was reading about it today—in a bookshop. Trying to find a cure for you. It said that. About the things that happen before.'

'It's weird.' Owen closed his eyes as if trying to recall the feeling.

'Are you hungry?' asked Michael.

'Starving.' Owen clicked his teeth together.

'Then I'll order you something to eat.' He said it in a posh voice. He picked up the telephone and raised his eyebrows as he thought a posh person would do, but when he spoke into the phone it was in his own voice. He apologized for being late but explained that he had mentioned it to the waitress earlier on. When he put the phone down they both laughed. A silence came between them. Still the rain rattled at the window in salvoes driven by the wind.

'Sounds a bit like the Home,' said Owen, nodding in the direction of the storm. Michael nodded. They both looked at the window and the reflection of the bedside lamp on it, flexing under the pressure of the gale.

'What do you mean by weird? The bit you remember?' Michael asked.

The boy paused, not knowing what to answer.

'Weird,' he said again.

'Like what?'

Owen thought for a long time. The deep thunder in the chimney continued.

'Do you know when you are writing on a blackboard—and the chalk slips—and you scrape your nail up against it?'

Michael gave an involuntary shudder.

'No. No, it's not like *that*. It's like that only it's *nice*.'

Owen moved his hands, trying to explain.

'It's like that only it's a *nice* feeling. Everything is right. Everything's in its right place ... it's the right colour, the right smell.

Sometimes I get a smell that . . . It's beautiful . . .'

The word coming from Owen sounded strange. The curtains stirred even though the windows were tight shut.

'The whole thing is . . . beautiful. I . . . I be happy. Just say . . . somebody who really *loves* the sound of his nails scratching down a blackboard, then that's what it's like. I be *that* happy.'

Owen stopped talking with a shrug and a twist of his mouth. They were both quiet.

'It sounds a bit daft,' said Michael eventually.

'It's hard to explain.'

'So it seems. But I think I understand what you're getting at.'

'I would like to be like that all the time,' said Owen. He sighed when he had said this and for a moment Michael saw him as a sick boy. The hard man image had fallen away from him and he lay back with his thin wrists upturned.

'A permanent fit?' said Michael.

The boy nodded.

'Sometimes I feel like that,' he said.

'Now?'

Owen smiled at him. 'No,' he said, 'not now.'

The bed creaked as Michael leaned back on to it.

'Right—let's say I'm your fairy godfather and I can grant you three wishes. What would they be?'

'A million quid and . . .'

'No—real things. Things you'd like to do.'

Owen thought, then said,

'To fly—'

'I said real, edgit.'

'—in a plane. That's real isn't it?'

'O.K.'

'—to be able to swim—eh,' he opened his mouth, thinking, '—to score for Arsenal at Wembley, and play the guitar.'

'That's four.'

'Well, then, my first wish would be to have four wishes.'

'Sneaky,' said Michael. 'But only one of them is real. The rest have to be taught. That involves work.'

'Not if you're a fairy godfather.'

'You're daft, son,' said Michael, smiling at him.

Another silence fell between them which lasted for some time. Michael broke it by telling him about the fugue. That people travel for weeks without knowing what's going on.

'We're a couple of fuguers,' he said, laughing again.

'Watch your language, Brother Sebastian.'

A round-up of the day's sport came on the radio and they heard that the Arsenal game had ended in a nil-all draw.

'We didn't miss much,' said Michael.

There was a knock at the door and when

Michael opened it, it was the old Irishwoman with a tray for Owen. She bustled in saying, 'Isn't that the terrible night out, Mr O'Leary?' She turned to Owen,

'And how is the wee man now?'

'Oh, he's much better,' said Michael, his hands out for the tray.

The woman walked past him and set the tray on Owen's knees. She fussed around him, fixing the pillows at his back.

'This boy needs fattening, Mr O'Leary. He's a rickle of bones. Do you like ham sandwiches?'

Owen nodded, biting into a neat triangle of bread. The woman poured his tea.

'And I brought a cup for you, Mr O'Leary. Will you have one?'

She had it poured already, and Michael took it rattling on its saucer. He wished she would go but she stood on, wanting to talk. She kept patting her white hair nervously. She wore the same cross-over flowered apron as before.

'On holiday, you say. Is Mrs O'Leary at home?'

'No. I'm afraid Mrs O'Leary is dead.' Michael fiddled with the ring on his finger.

'Oh, I'm sorry to hear that. He'll be an only child then?' she said, nodding towards the boy. 'And you'll be wanting to know where you'll get mass in the morning?' Owen made a slurping noise drinking his tea.

'Eh? Yes. With all the fuss I'd forgotten tomorrow was Sunday,' said Michael.

'Well you haven't too far to go. Just round the corner, to your right. The big church on the right. There's masses on the hour right up till one o'clock for the lazy ones.'

The sports programme ended and some pop music came on the radio. Michael leaned over and turned the sound up.

'You like this one, Owen, don't you?'

The old woman had to raise her voice to speak now.

'Can you get Radio Eireann on it?'

'Yes.'

'I can get it on mine too. I like to keep up with what's happening at home. This trouble in the North is terrible.'

'Yes, awful.'

'And this kidnapping business. Have you heard about that?'

The old woman was looking him straight in the eye. Michael stared back at her, not wanting to seem guilty. He sat down on the bed.

'I think I heard it mentioned the other day.'

'It was on every day for near a week there. A man about your age and a boy. It's terrible what some people get up to.'

'Yes, isn't it.'

The woman was still looking at him.

'What part of Swords did you say you lived?'

'Out the Dublin road. Hey, listen to this one, Owen.'

An old Beatles song came on. 'All You Need

133

is Love.' Michael stood up and began to back the woman towards the door.

'He's mad keen on the music,' he said. The woman retreated a few steps, realizing now that she wasn't wanted. She was still staring at his face as if she wanted to memorize it as she left the room.

'How long did you say you'd be staying?' she asked.

'A couple of days,' said Michael, 'Oh, and leave the tray until the morning. We'll be going to sleep shortly.'

'Good night,' she said. 'Sleep tight.'

When the door was closed and she had had time to get to the end of the corridor Michael switched off the radio and said,

'She knows.'

Owen stopped chewing.

'I'm sure she suspects us, Owen. The question is whether to get out tonight or first thing in the morning.'

CHAPTER THIRTEEN

Because of the weather and because he knew the difficulty of getting a new hotel at that time of night with a sick boy on his hands, Michael for once decided to trust his luck. It was better than walking the streets or spending such a night in one of the railway stations. He lay awake listening to the wind and tensed every time quiet footsteps traversed the carpeted corridor. When someone had gone past the door, the handle gave a tiny vibration and Michael relaxed again. The footsteps and the singing of the plumbing eventually stopped but he could not sleep. Everything became exaggerated. He could not only hear the ticking of a clock but the turning of the mechanism inside. The bed irritated him at all points of contact; he itched and tickled but was too intent on sleeping to scratch. Towards morning the storm died to blade-light whistles. The room began to take on a ghostly outline of its shape, the greyness seeping through the curtains. Somewhere a blackbird startled into song and was joined by others, starlings, sparrows. Michael pulled the pillow over his ears and clenched his eyes tightly shut. Ever since he could remember he had hated this alarm call of the birds.

In this state, as the room moved from darkness to light, the glimmerings of a plan came into his mind. He had fought so hard for the past few hours rejecting thoughts and images that had appeared like demons to torment him that he gave up and let the plan stay. It was terrible in its implications. He hoped it was the result of a night's depression and insomnia and that it would disappear with the light of day, like the tingling and the itch.

It was an idea which was easy to conceive,

but he seriously doubted that he would have the courage to carry it through. When it had first occurred to him his face had broken into a smile in the darkness, it seemed so ludicrous. But as the night went on, the idea would not leave him alone. It came to him from cul-de-sacs, popped up and leered at him from behind the screens he put up. Spoke to him of plausibility. The smile died on his face and as the hours ticked on the plan became the only possible drastic solution. It was motivated by love. It would be a pure act. Of this he was sure.

He knew he was depressed but could do nothing about it. His limbs were of lead but his mind whirred on through endless, hopeless repetitions of the same idea. There was no way out for them, either Owen or himself.

He knew, too, and he could not give a reason for it, that they would have to return to Ireland. In this country among strangers the act would have no meaning for him. He felt homesickness repeat on him like acid. And yet he could not think of a single thing he regretted leaving. What he did know was that there was nothing to hold him here, among these crowds with their English clacking tongues. Pagan England, his father had called it.

They would fly. It would be a way of using up what money was left. Another phrase of his father's. To get things used up. It was the reason he gave for most things. Eating and drinking and drawing on paper bags. Everything had to be used up. One of Owen's wishes had been to fly. Michael could grant it. Brother Benedict had told him his name, Michael, was from the Hebrew, meaning 'who is like God?' Grant it, O Lord. Let us fly.

In the plan was their salvation. He wanted this to be his one positive act. All his life he had been doing negative things, obedient things under pressure of religion and human respect. This was one decision he had arrived at by *himself*. Or at least he thought he had. Ten years ago, on such a night as this, he would have assumed it was God talking to him. There seemed no doubt that someone was putting his foot in the door. Selling him something he did not at first want to buy. No matter how often he changed the subject, the same patter came back. Now that he had ceased to believe in God he wondered who or what was pounding at him. Perhaps it was himself or a part of himself that he refused to recognize. He allowed it finally to be his own decision.

He swung himself out of bed and saw that the time was six-thirty. There was only one thing that could save him from the plan and that was going to Maguire, the solicitor. Michael collected all the money he had from various pockets and his store from the back of the drawer. He knew roughly how much he

137

had but he had to check to make sure it was as bad as he thought. He pulled the curtains apart a slit to give himself more light and began to work out sums in his cash book. He had just enough to carry out his plan with a little extra for luxuries.

It now depended on Maguire. He dressed quietly and picked up all the loose change from beside the notes and slipped out of the room. The hotel was bright and quiet. In the foyer he heard distant noises and voices from the kitchen. He went to the telephone with the perspex hood and dialled the number. He piled the column of his tenpences on the shelf. Maguire would be mad, being phoned at this time of the morning. If he was home at all. Michael heard the quiet rhythmic purr of the dialling tone. When he heard the pips he put his money in.

'Hello? Mr Maguire?'

'Who is it?' snapped Maguire's voice. 'Do you realize the time?'

'Yes. I'm very sorry. Did I get you out of bed?'

'Yes. And it's bloody well Sunday.'

'This is Michael Lamb here.'

'Who?' The voice was high-pitched with irritation.

'Michael Lamb. My father died some weeks ago and we came to an arrangement about his will.'

'Yes, I know rightly who you are. What do

138

you want?'

'You remember I had some money left?'

'I don't think so.'

'You said it was roughly two thousand . . .' A cleaning woman passed carrying a Hoover and Michael stopped talking until she was out of earshot. 'And you gave me eight hundred, so that leaves something, doesn't it?'

'You are in no position to bargain, Mr Lamb . . .'

Pip pip pip pip pip pip.

Michael fumbled with his money and put another tenpence in the slot.

Maguire's voice came back: 'You're in no position to bargain. Where are you anyway?'

'That's not important.'

'How can I send the money to you? By the way, this is not a kidnap demand, is it?'

'Don't be silly.'

'Is the boy all right?'

'Of course he is.'

'Where can I contact you?'

Michael hesitated.

'Can I trust you?' he said.

'Sure. Just wait till I get a pencil.'

Michael kicked himself for his own stupidity. He had forgotten that to get the money he would have to reveal his whereabouts. If he used a postal address it would be watched until he picked the money up. If he went to Maguire himself he would certainly shop him to the police and pocket the money. He was sure Maguire was going to pocket the money no matter what happened. If he could catch a criminal into the bargain it would look well for him.

'Hello. Righty-ho. Fire ahead,' said Maguire's voice.

Pip pip pip pip.

Michael put the phone down.

He stood and noticed that his knees were shaking. His plan would have to go ahead. It was the only way. With a heart of lead, he climbed the stairs, each one an individual effort.

Money was at the root of the whole problem. Money could save them now for a while. If Owen had been born into a family which had not had to live on the borders of poverty for most of the time, then the situation would not have arisen. One of Owen's dodges had been to stop tourists on the street and offer to say three Hail Marys for them for five pence. Many showed him the back of their hand, but many paid to hear his accent and for the quaintness of the custom. He gave as little as possible of this money into the house but his mother knew the turnover and he had to give some. The luck to be born into such a family. What was needed now was a few even breaks to counteract the accumulated ill-luck of years. The old Irish woman didn't seem to have informed on them. He wakened Owen.

'Come on, I think our luck's held,' he said.

They got dressed and Michael packed their bag. This time they had to leave the toys and the model plane, now almost completely assembled. Owen was loath to leave the toys but he just shrugged at the loss of the plane. Michael allowed him to keep two small things and he chose the gun and sheath knife to pack in the bag. In a small café with its seats arranged all along one side like horse boxes they had breakfast, in silence. Everything rattled loudly on the Formica surface of the table. There was a fat plastic tomato with ketchup congealed around its nozzle, and Michael slid it behind the menu. An Indian lady with an apron over her sari served them. She had a small red exclamation mark between her eyebrows.

When they had finished Michael said,

'We can make eight o'clock mass somewhere if you hurry.'

'Aw no,' said Owen, screwing up his face.

'It's Sunday.'

'I thought you said you'd forget about *everything*.'

'There are some things you shouldn't forget about.'

'It's crap. Preachin' and all.'

'Some of it is,' Michael agreed. 'But not all of it.' He consulted his *A-Z* and circled the nearest church with the pen Owen had nicked for him.

'Will you go to communion?' asked Michael.

'If you say so.'

'No. Can you go to communion?'

'Yeah.'

'Are you sure?'

'I've done nothing. Sure I'm sure.'

'Good,' said Michael, 'I just wanted to know.'

The church looked near in the *A-Z*, but it was ten past eight by the time they arrived. It was a large dark Gothic building with stained-glass windows which were so dirty that they let in little light. It was like a church at night. Michael and Owen knelt down in their seat about half way up the church. The priest who was reading the psalm was obviously Irish. He was very old.

'"Save me, O God,"' his voice quavered, '"for the waters threaten my life. I am sunk in the abysmal swamp where there is no foothold; I have reached the watery depths; the flood overwhelms me. I am wearied with calling, my throat is parched . . ."' At this point the old priest took a fit of coughing and Owen laughed up at Michael.

'"My eyes have failed with looking for my God. Those outnumber the hairs of my head who hate me without cause."'

'He's baldy,' hissed Owen, still laughing.

'Cut it out. We didn't come here to make fun.'

'"Too many for my strength are they who wrongfully are my enemies. Must I restore

142

what I did not steal?"'

They stood for the gospel and then sat for the sermon.

Michael felt the lack of a night's sleep catching up on him. His eyes were heavy and the lids kept coming together. Once his head pitched forward and he woke.

The sermon was something about the early Christians, how they were persecuted and had to form secret societies. They used as a sign *Icthus*, meaning fish. Owen leaned over to Michael:

'Is that the bloke we were reading about?'

'Who?'

'The guy that made the wings?'

'No. That was Icarus.'

'Pardon my iggerance,' and he laughed too loud.

'Shhh.'

The Brothers were a bit like a secret society but they were neither fish nor fowl, neither lay nor fully clerical. The half-collar they wore was an indication of their status. When they had come recruiting to his school—'for fishers of men'—all those years ago and had offered the glittering lures of sanctity and safety, Michael had jumped selflessly.

It was a long time before the line pulled taut and he felt the pain of the hooks within him and the irony of the fisherman caught.

Owen nudged him again.

'There's eighteen here,' he said.

143

'What?'

'Only eighteen people—and they're all old.'

'Pay attention.'

Pay attention. Michael smiled within himself. What did it matter? There was a time when it did. 'Must I restore what I did not steal?' The phrase hung on in his mind like weed snagged on a stick while the rest of it washed away. Here he was trying to force Owen to accept what he no longer believed in. But when he had been that age he had believed totally and absolutely, and on reflection the advantages had outweighed the disadvantages.

The guilt of his sins, the bad thoughts, the touching himself, had to be set against the warmth and security of having in his mind a Christ figure that loved him, that he could talk to intimately and as he believed then, who would listen to him. It was nice to be forgiven for something bad that he had done, to come back to Jesus saying: I am sorry for having offended You, I love You so much that I will never sin again. And the tears would be on the brink of his eyes with the beauty of it all. Love. Jesus. Him. Imaginary companions. His loving father.

He had loved the hymns. That feeling they gave him of prickles down his neck when the whole congregation stood and sang at the tops of their voices:

Blood of My Saviour
Bathe me in thy tide,
Wash me in waters
Streaming from His side.

The church vibrated with the sound. His father had a good voice, like someone on the radio, and it rose above the others and Michael was proud he was his father. The only one who wasn't in the church was his mother. He had to save everything up to tell her when he got home from devotions. A bit of the sermon, what hymns they had sung, had anyone taken ill, had a priest thumped the pulpit, had he got the rosary exact, saying ten Hail Marys, not nine or eleven as he was wont to do.

He no longer believed in any of it. Faith was a bit like luck. Spiritual luck. By the end of his novitiate it had begun to drain away. He struggled and prayed to retain it but each morning that he awoke he realized that he had less of it. He had sprung a leak and he didn't know where to mend it.

Nevertheless he took his final vows. He did not know what else he could do. To back out at that stage would have killed his father. He was convinced of it.

Once he had discussed the problem with his Novice Master but he had averted his face and told him to pray. After this his prayers carried an extra phrase—if You exist. God, if You exist, help me. But this compromise eventually gave way to not praying at all. He felt totally trapped. The strange thing that he found was that he was still the same person, his actions remained just as moral, his desire to be fully Christian was still there. Love was what governed all he did. It was funny in a way that it was his love for his father and a desire not to hurt him that kept him for so long in the Brothers. But when his father died everything changed.

God forgive me, thought Michael, but it was lucky he died when he did. It gave me a chance. How different Owen would have been if he had had a father like mine. The whole thing was like a lottery. Owen draws a father who beats him, a mother who hates him. The odds are all against him. Would I have been the same as him if I had been born into a family like this?

Would he have been the same as me, with my parents?

Prayer was for fighting bad luck. If the prayer did not succeed then you had to accept the bad luck as the will of God. Please God, let me pass my examinations. Fail. I accept Your holy will. Pray for a miracle.

Miracles were good luck, if they ever happened. For some. Christ came to the man bound in fetters who was howling and gnashing and drove the devils out of him into a herd of swine. Then they all ran into the sea and were drowned. Good luck for the man in the fetters.

Not so hot for the man who owned the swine.

He imagined his father applying to the Government for compensation.

'Well, you see, there was this fella came into town the other night and . . .'

'What are you smiling at?' asked Owen.

'Never mind.'

He knew that his concept of God was old-fashioned. He tried to replace it with something not so naïve, to see if that would work. God is love. But that slipped through his fingers, gave him no purchase and he was left with: I am love. If God ceased to exist tomorrow there would be enough love in every individual to keep the whole thing going, to make it worthwhile. Just so long as people like his father continued to be born, then it would be all right.

Thousands of saviours like his father in any one lifetime would be sufficient fuel for the world. They must exist. He knew because he was one of them himself. He knew he was good. I am love. There was no pride or pomposity in this thought for him. He just knew that he wanted to help in whatever way he could the suffering of the world. In the world was better. Of people in the world. Of Owen. Brother Benedict was right—he could not think.

The old priest shuffled through his mass on an altar that was an island of light in the gloom of the church.

'Lamb of God, who takest away the sins of the world, grant us peace.' His bald head shone as he stooped to receive the host. The feet of the others scraped emptily as they made their way to the altar. Michael received communion with Owen as he had done many times before, but this time he felt guilty. He was deceiving the boy. Would it not be better to tell him the truth of what he believed or disbelieved? The trouble was that he couldn't put it into words to tell anybody, let alone explain it to a child. Children copied the people they liked and Owen would follow him into his fog of unbelief without a moment's hesitation.

Michael peeled the host from the roof of his mouth with his tongue and swallowed it. He bent over as if praying, and stayed like that until mass finished.

The priest had gone off the altar but the old congregation sat on. A woman in front of them wore a hat that looked as if it was made of brains, convoluted grey material. She whistled her prayers and Owen started to make fun of her, making a noise like calling a cat. *Pss-wshhh-wshhh*.

'Come on,' said Michael.

In the porch on a table beside an empty collection plate were some *Irish Weeklys*. Michael bought one and left the right money. He opened the inside leaves of the paper and saw a photograph of Owen staring out at him. He rustled it shut.

148

'Let's get out of here,' he said. They walked quickly away from the church and saw a park.

'Wait till you see this,' said Michael sitting down on the grass.

'What?'

Michael showed him his picture. He was thrilled.

'Hey . . .' was all he could say. 'Me in the paper.'

Michael read him the caption: 'Boy still missing', and the story.

'That means we'll have to stop being Catholics,' Michael said.

'How so?'

'Well this paper is sold to the Irish all over and they're Catholics. They'll see your picture. I bet you that oul' woman in the hotel will see it. We didn't leave there a minute too soon.'

'Yeah.'

'I bet you she'll phone the police this morning. We may say goodbye to London, Owney.'

'I don't care. Where to next?'

'Last night I was thinking. I couldn't sleep and I thought of a sort of a plan. Where is the last place they would think of looking for us?'

Owen thought for a while.

'Japan,' he guessed.

'No, y'egit. Seriously. Where?'

'I don't know,' he said, giving up.

'In Ireland,' said Michael. 'The word is out that they are looking for us here and if that

149

woman phones then they definitely will look for us here. Nobody will think of looking for us at home.'

Owen was not sure. He said, 'But not too close to *the* Home?'

'No.'

There was a long silence between them. Owen obviously wanted to say something but found it difficult. Then he came out with it.

'You're not thinking of handing me in, are you?'

Michael was taken aback. He laughed and put his arms about the boy.

'No, Owney. Do you not trust me even yet?'

'That's O.K. then.'

'O.K., Owen Kane,' said Michael. 'Would you like to fly?'

The boy's face lit up.

'Smashin',' he said. He got up off the grass, stretched his arms out at his shoulders and made a whining noise like a jet as he ran round and round Michael. Then he ran out of steam and plunged down beside him, a rumpled heap on the grass.

CHAPTER FOURTEEN

It took them most of the day getting the whole way across London and when they arrived at the airport they were told that the next flight to

150

Belfast was on Monday. Michael spent twenty minutes on the phone trying to find a hotel for the night.

The windows in their room were double-glazed and it was Owen who noticed the dead flies that lay on the sill between the glass. It was by far the best hotel they had stayed in. Their room had a colour television and a radio and a private bathroom. There was even a current *Radio Times* and *T.V. Times* to tell them what programmes were on that night.

They had a meal and Owen couldn't leave the table quick enough to get back up to the television. He asked Michael to buy him cigarettes and a big Coke, and then ran to the lift.

Michael stood at the bar waiting to be served. Through the crowd he saw a girl watching him from the opposite end of the bar. She seemed to be watching him through the noise. Michael looked away then back at her again. She was still watching him and when he looked back at her for a third time she smiled at him. Michael felt himself getting embarrassed. She was too good-looking for him.

Eventually he was served with his cigarettes and as a sort of afterthought he bought himself a half pint of bitter. He drank it standing and occasionally looked over at the girl. She was dark-haired, hair that fell in a tumble to her shoulders. Her eyes were dark brown and occasionally she gnawed delicately at the painted nail of her little finger. Before he left she smiled at him again.

Going up in the lift he remembered reading somewhere that the lines in television pictures could set off a fit in an epileptic. He went into the room. Owen had the curtains pulled and an armchair drawn up to the set. The place was dark except for the flickering colours as each scene changed. Michael opened the cigarettes and offered the boy one. He took it without saying a word or taking his eyes off the screen. Michael struck a match for him.

'What is it?' he asked.

'Songs of Praise,' said Owen.

'Anything good on later?'

'Yeah.'

'What is it?'

'A Western. *Piaowoooo, piaowooooo,*' he made two noises at the back of his throat. 'John Wayne.'

Michael went out to the bathroom and pulled the cord light. He took out his shaving gear.

'Did the doctor ever tell you anything about watching the T.V.?' he shouted.

'No.'

'Come on. Did he?'

'He said if I feel funny I've to cover one eye.'

'How do you feel?'

'O.K.'

Michael lathered all round his beard and began carefully to shave his cheeks. He straightened off the line at his cheeks, at his sideburns and underneath his neck. He washed and dried his face and inspected himself in the mirror. He was pleased with the result. It now looked more like a beard than a growth. He changed his shirt and put on some after-shave. He slipped off his wedding ring and left it on the bathroom shelf.

'Will you be all right on your own? I'm going down to the bar.'

Owen did not answer but Michael saw his head move up and down. A minister in a white surplice and half-moon glasses came on the screen.

'If you feel funny, cover one eye,' said Michael as he left.

When he got to the bar he was disappointed to see that it had emptied and that the girl was gone. Two couples sat at opposite ends of the room. It was quiet enough to hear the Musak. Michael debated whether or not to go back to his room and watch the Western with Owney. But he needed to be away from the boy. He went out of the hotel and walked to find a place where more was happening so that it might stop his mind from racing.

In a side street he saw several lit neon signs. He went into the first bar he came to. It was an old-fashioned pub, smoke-filled and crowded with men talking. It reminded him of pubs at home and at once he felt comfortable. While he drank his first pint he concentrated on looking at the ornate carvings on the mahogany behind the bar. On the partition close to him he could see the tracks of the chisel. When he ordered his second pint a man sitting on a stool along from him spoke.

'I've heard that accent before,' he said.

Michael smiled at him, unsure whether the remark had been friendly or not.

'What part of Ireland are you from?'

'Dublin.'

'Christ, they're in some mess over there. Smoke?' He offered Michael a cigarette.

'No, thanks.'

The man was about the same age as Michael, slightly built with black, corrugated hair to his shoulders. He had a dark drooping moustache.

'Yes, it's tragic,' said Michael. 'It doesn't affect us too much in the South. It's the North that's really bad.'

'You don't have to tell me, mate. I've been there.'

'Army?'

The man looked at him closely. He seemed not drunk, but had been drinking.

'No. Business. Are you on holiday?'

Michael echoed him.

'No. Business,' and they both smiled.

'Can I buy you a drink, sur?' The man made a passable imitation of Michael's accent.

Michael did not want to be drawn into his company but the man forced him to have another pint. He was friendly and seemed to laugh at everything, not scornfully but because he found it genuinely funny. For a moment or two Michael forgot about the mood he was in while he listened to the jokes and stories of the other man. He had not heard any of them before and some he did not fully understand but laughed all the same. The man introduced himself as Haddock and Michael said his name was O'Leary. They shook hands.

'What was your business in Northern Ireland?' Michael asked.

Haddock hesitated.

'Photography,' he said. 'What's your business here?'

'No. I'm only joking. I don't have a job.'

'That's what I like to hear,' said Haddock, throwing his hair back from his face with his hand. 'I hate these bastards who spend their lives working. They talk about progress. The fuckin' cavemen had it right. They knew. An afternoon's work killing a dinosaur and live off it for a couple of weeks. When the two-hour fortnight comes in I might get a job myself.'

'How do you live then?'

'The State provides for most of my needs and I've a few other things going, besides. I drink as much as I can so I don't eat much. I live free in a nice little squat around the corner.'

155

'A what?'

'A squat. Round the corner from 'ere. A house that's earmarked for demolition. Some of us fixed it up a bit and moved in. Cost nothing.'

They talked for a time, both men hedging on the Northern Ireland issue. They had several rounds of drinks and, after Michael declared his loathing of all factions of the war in Ulster, Haddock admitted that he had been in the Army.

'What a life that was. No disrespect, mate, but I hate your fucking country. I hate the British Army an' all. Nobody was ever meant to live like that. Do this, do that, kiss my arse. I swore that when I got out of it I'd never take an order from anyone again, whether he was in uniform or not.'

'Is that why you don't work?'

'No. It's because I'm a lazy bastard.' He laughed loudly. 'It's all the same to me. I don't give a shit one way or the other. I'm free to do as I like. Two more pints, love,' he called.

The beer was beginning to have its effect. Michael felt himself become talkative but wanted to guard against saying too much. He was acting jovially but inside him the plan still tainted everything.

'This squat place,' he said, 'are there many more houses like it?' He was clutching at straws.

'Mick, London is full of them. They're all

over. Why do you ask?'

'I might be looking for a place. I'm not sure. I don't have a lot of money.'

Haddock reached out his hand and laid it on his shoulder.

'Then look no further,' he said. 'There's a space in our house at this very minute.'

'I'd have to get a job.'

'Fuck the job. Just collect the dole.'

'It's not as simple as that. There could be complications.'

'Like what?'

Michael thought for a moment, then said, 'I have a boy with me.'

'A boy?'

'Yes. Owen. We need a place together.'

'No trouble. Why don't you come round and see it? It might do you in the meantime.'

'Do you really mean that?' Michael was trying to gauge just how drunk Haddock was. 'I might just do that.'

'You must.'

Michael bought one for the road. His spirits soared. He laughed and warmed to Haddock, wanting to hug him. The taint evaporated. Here was an opening. He could scrap the plan, get himself a job, have Owen with him. They might *never* be found. It didn't matter what the place was like, it would have to do.

On the street Michael staggered a bit and Haddock put his arm around his shoulder to steady him. He let his arm stay there but

Michael eased himself out from under it. Haddock faced away from him and said,

'Are you straight?'

'What do you mean?'

'Are you gay?'

'No,' said Michael unsurely. 'No. I'm not.'

'Every cripple has his own way of walking,' said Haddock. 'Freedom for all. What about the boy?'

'He's my son.'

Haddock said nothing but started laughing, holding the top of his head with both hands. He continued to snigger, on and off, until they reached the house. Because he said the front was boarded up they went in at the back door. Haddock laughed and said,

'I always think that's significant, when you consider who lives here.'

He stooped and from somewhere produced a bicycle lamp. Its circle of light wobbled across only half a floor. A board was laid across the open joints to the foot of the stairs.

'Careful. Keep to the plank,' said Haddock. Michael tight-roped unsteadily across it. Two flights up the floor was better.

Haddock showed him the room he could have. There was a mattress in the corner and a deck-chair with candy-striped canvas. The walls were covered in posters, there was a thread bare rug on the floor and on the one window a sagging curtain of unknown colour on a string. Haddock directed the lamp on to a wastepaper tin full to overflowing. When he bent over his hair covered his face.

'Needs a bit of tidyin', if you like that sort of thing.'

Cigarette butts and fat, used tea-bags and papers that spilled on to the floor. Most of the papers were the wrappings of camomile tea. There was a strange odour in the room and Michael did not know whether it was pleasant or not.

'It'll look fine wiv a bit of imagination,' said Haddock. He struck a match and lit a candle stub stuck to a tin lid. From this he lit a cigarette. 'It's yours if you want it,' he said. 'The bloke who was here just cleared out about a week ago. Said he was going to India. Just like that.' Michael thought for a moment. The alternative seemed so final that he knew he had no option.

'O.K.. Thanks. We'll try it. We'll come tomorrow.'

The yellow candle flame wobbled in a draught as a man opened the door.

'Oh, it's you,' he said. The voice was negroid and light. Vexed.

'This is my Nutan,' said Haddock. 'He shares with me.'

'Shit, man,' said Nutan.

'Hold on, will ya,' shouted Haddock. 'This is—I've forgot your name.'

'Michael.'

'Michael. He's moving in 'ere.'

'Yo'r shit,' said Nutan to Haddock.

'He's moving in with a boy of his own.'

Nutan was dressed in a tight turquoise polo-neck with a black medallion of some sort round his neck. He looked about eighteen, tall and thin with Afro-style hair and a gold hoop ear-ring. He said nothing more but went back across the landing to his room. He slammed the door.

'He's very touchy sometimes,' said Haddock.

'Will it be all right?'

'Sure. He'll be all over you tomorrow. He's a nice fella really. And Keith and Barry upstairs are O.K. too.'

'I'd better be getting back.'

'I'll show you the kitchen on the way down.'

At the back door Michael stopped and shook hands with Haddock.

'And thanks again.'

'Don't mention it. Someday you can do the same for me. We're all in it together, Paddy. See ya.' He shouted after him, 'Better bring a light and a few cups and things.'

The drink and the change of circumstance made Michael feel better than he had for weeks. He now had hope for the future again. A fighting chance. He walked quickly and looked up to see the sky but could see nothing because of the street lights. All the way back to the hotel, in the dark eaves of the buildings above his head starlings chittered.

When he got back to the hotel he went to check how Owen was. The boy had switched the television off and was sitting on the bed crying.

'You big bastard. Where were you?' Owen screamed. He jumped up and began to punch at Michael. Michael bent down to try and pinion his arms in a kind of embrace, but a fist struck him on the lip.

'Easy, easy, Owen,' he said. 'What's the matter?'

'Where were you? I thought you'd run away from me.'

'Never, never. I just went for a walk with a bloke.'

The boy stopped struggling, but stayed in Michael's arms.

'You took the fags with you.' Owen was giving little shudders after his long bout of crying. 'I went down to the bar to get them from you but you weren't there. I thought you'd run away.'

'Look, Owen, I love you. I will not run away from you because I love you. You must trust me. Anyway, I've got some good news for you.'

'What?'

'We've got a place to stay—for good.' Michael held him at arm's length to see the reaction on his face. There was none. But then the boy had no idea that he had been spared the plan, no idea that the money was so low. To him it was just another move.

'Where?' he asked.

'Not far from here.'

'For good?'

'Until we get something better.'

'Then we're not going to fly?' His voice was still snagging after the tears.

'No—sorry about that. But it can't be helped.'

'What's it like?'

'A bit grotty. It's a room in a house that's going to be knocked down in a year or two. It's full of weirdos, but that shouldn't affect us.'

'What kind of weirdos?'

'Freaky weirdos,' said Michael and they both laughed. He hugged him close, the boy's face against his chest. The boy hugged him back and he felt the salt taste of blood on his lips.

CHAPTER FIFTEEN

This was the easiest move of all because they only had their original bag left. When Michael settled the bill he made a roll of the tenners left and put it away in his 'untouchable pocket'. For the rainy day. He thought for a moment, then took two ten-pound notes out and put them with his other money. They would need things.

When they reached the house, Owen walked

the plank with the bag slung across his shoulders and once upstairs he immediately sat in the deck-chair.

'This is just like home,' he said, laughing. 'Crap.'

Michael chugged the curtain open. In the daylight the place looked even more bleak than it had the night before.

'Let's get to work on it then.'

There was no sign of Haddock or any of the others. In the fireplace Michael made a fire of the papers and cigarette packets. He used a piece of cardboard to sweep up all the rubbish. The fire blazed briefly and Owen pulled his deck-chair up close to it.

'Do some work,' said Michael.

'What is there to do?'

Michael went down to the kitchen and soaked a handkerchief and gave it to Owen to get some of the dirt off the window. He made a list of things they would need. A torch, a quilt, cups, some food. He asked Owen for suggestions.

'Coal. Let's get one of those wee bags of coal and have a fire, eh?'

The papers had burnt out and were now black and feathery, stirring in the draught. Tiny beads of red appeared here and there on them.

They went shopping together and came back laden, Owen barely able to see where he was going from behind the box of the quilt.

Still there was no sign of Haddock. Michael got a good fire blazing in the grate and made beans, fried chopped ham and bread, and they sat listening to Radio One on the transistor, eating with their fingers, their feet in the hearth.

'This is smashin',' said Owen. 'Better'n a hotel any day.'

Michael nodded, his mouth full.

Just then they heard a footstep outside and the door opened. It was Haddock.

'I wondered who it was,' he said.

He stood, his hands in his pockets, his face still puffy with sleep. He seemed different from the previous night.

'Well, we're here,' said Michael.

'So I see.'

'This is Owen.'

'Hi,' said Haddock. 'I had too much to drink last night.'

Michael wiped up the last of his bean juice with his bread.

'You want tea?' he asked.

'Don't let the fuzz see that boy coming in here,' said Haddock. 'He's under age.'

He turned and left, yawning and scratching his head with both hands.

That night they slept on the single mattress, snug under the quilt, watching the last of the flames flickering on the ceiling. Michael explained to Owen why he would have to get a job if they were going to have any sort of

164

permanence in this set-up. Owen agreed but didn't fancy the idea much. They would have to try it for a week to see if it worked. Owen yawned and Michael followed him. He could get a job on a building site somewhere, give a false name. He could say he had never worked in England before.

'Grandma and me used to make spoons,' said Owen.

So they 'made spoons', Owen bending his knees and Michael slotting into his shape.

'You're all bones,' said Michael. He put his arm around him and eventually they fell asleep.

The next day Michael took Owen with him and they spent most of the day job hunting. He described himself as a carpenter and got a job on a site about six miles away from the squat. Owen waited for him on the pavement while he went to see the foreman.

They bought an alarm clock and pencils and jotters to help Owen pass the time while Michael was away. He set him an essay to write about the Home. That night he made sandwiches and wrapped them in tin foil to keep them fresh for Owen's lunch. He wondered about the fire and in the end told Owen not to light it. There was no other way he could damage himself, even if he had a fit. He warned him to take his tablets.

Earlier, while he had been in the kitchen, he had met Barry and Keith. They both wore coats with straggly hair like goat beards round the hems. They were drunk or on drugs and staggered about the place laughing. From their talk he gathered they were on drugs. He felt distinctly uneasy with these two and was glad that Owen was upstairs. As they prepared their meal they kept goosing each other and whooping with mock surprise and embarrassment. They were both talking like 'nice boys' and flapping their hands about.

In the morning the alarm rang and he left Owen sleeping. There were a number of Irishmen working on the site and during the morning tea break they asked him a lot of awkward questions, so at lunchtime he avoided them and worked through the next tea break. Not being used to a full day's physical labour, he was totally exhausted when five o'clock came. It was well after six by the time he got back to the squat.

When he went into the room he was surprised to find Haddock being friendly again. He stood by the fireplace, his hand on his hip.

'Wotcha, mate,' he said.

Owen was sitting on the mattress.

'Hello,' said Michael. 'How did you get on today, Owen?'

'O.K.'

'He was fine,' said Haddock. 'Just fine. We got on well together, didn't we?'

'Where's your friend?' asked Michael.

'Nutan? He works. Keeps me in pocket money.'

There was a strange undefinable sweetish smell in the room. Haddock was wearing a lime green scarf knotted about his neck.

'I see you're settling nicely,' he said.

'Yes, thanks again. It solved our problems just at the right time.'

When Haddock had gone Michael lay down on the bed, his hands cupped behind his head. He said.

'Well, how did you pass the day?'

'Smoking . . . talking . . . eating. I was bored, then he came in.

'Did you do any writing?'

'A bit. But your man told me not to bother.'

'He did, did he?'

'Said it was a crap idea.'

'Well I give the orders around here. I'm the captain. You do it tomorrow.'

Michael felt on edge. He put it down to tiredness and hunger but basically he knew it was about this place. Haddock had not actually done anything yet, but Michael knew that he was capable of it. His euphoria of the previous day had gone. The drink that he had taken the night he met Haddock had suppressed any misgivings he had had about the man. Sober and unsmiling, Haddock had a lean and sly look about him. Slimy. But what could Michael do? He couldn't take the boy to work with him, neither could he let him roam the streets all day—he would be sure to get lost or have an attack somewhere awkward. Haddock was as queer as a fourpenny piece. But queers were all right. He didn't think he had met one before. You could leave a little girl with a man and that would be all right—most times. Would it be the same with Owen and Haddock? Would the consequences of 'wait and see' be worth it? How would it affect the boy if Haddock tried something indescribable? His mind swivelled away from the thought.

'I don't think this is going to work out,' he said.

'Why not?'

'I don't like leaving you alone for so long. Anything could happen.'

'Haddock is here all day.'

For a while Michael said nothing. Then, 'That's what I'm afraid of.'

'He's a laugh.'

'Maybe,' said Michael. 'I'm going to get something to eat.'

He heaved himself to his feet, his bones creaking, and went down to the kitchen. And yet Haddock could be useful to them, maybe. He was what Michael imagined a small-time crook to be. He seemed to know his way around the regulations, social security regulations and the like. Perhaps after a week or so he could help fix them up with a new identity—and Owen could go to school, come September, with no questions asked. They

168

would live on here until he had gathered enough money to get a real place on a permanent basis.

But the next day he went to work with the conviction that it was pointless. They could not go on living like this. The previous night Owen and he had barely spoken and anything that Michael had said had been irritable. He had gone to bed shortly after nine o'clock and fallen asleep immediately. To leave the boy in that house for ten or eleven hours was asking for trouble. All day as he worked his mind went back to the plan and he hated himself for it. But the alternative was too awful to consider. That the boy should return to the Home and then after, maybe, years go back to his totally inadequate and snivelling mother and live with her in some Dublin slum. Since they had run away together, Owen had tasted freedom and, Michael hoped, love, and it would be doubly difficult to return to the warping influence and viciousness of Benedict and the taunts and sneers of the older boys. Owen was without a future—either way. But Michael's way had something to recommend it. Owen's mother hated him. She had tried to kill him. The thought lodged in Michael's mind like a fishbone in his throat and all day as he worked he was conscious of it. She had tried to kill Owen from hate.

He knew he was sliding back into his depression and could get no purchase anywhere to prevent himself.

That night when he crossed the plank he heard pop music from the transistor in their room. If Haddock was there again he knew he would get angry. He opened the door and went in. Haddock was sitting on the mattress with his arm around Owen's shoulders. He was wearing a red silk dressing gown and his bent knee stuck whitely out of it. Owen was sucking on a loose, soggy cigarette.

'The breadwinner is back,' said Haddock and let his head roll to one side.

'What are you doing?' Michael was incredulous.

'Smoking,' said Owen. His words were slurred and his eyes were heavy-lidded. The air had that sweetish smell in it.

'Smoking what?'

'Pot,' said Haddock. 'The best of shit.'

'What?' Michael walked over to them and took the cigarette off Owen and threw it in the fireplace. 'Don't let me catch you at that again. And as for you, Haddock, I've never heard anything so ... so incredible. Teaching a boy of his age.'

'Jesus, Paddy, you sound like my mother.'

'Will you stop calling me Paddy? Get out before I hit you.'

Haddock put his hands up defensively.

'Doctors say there's no harm in it.' He took his arm from around Owen's shoulders. 'We had a nice time, didn't we, Owen?' He got up awkwardly.

'Indeedwedid.' Owen ran the words together.

'Heard a few *interesting* things, too,' said Haddock.

Michael bunched his fists and faced Haddock, who moved past him smiling. When he walked his bare leg came out of his dressing gown. He sang, 'Brother, can you spare a dime?' softly as he went to the door.

Michael followed him. Outside he spun him by the shoulder.

'Did you touch that boy?'

'Now, Paddy, would oi do a ting like dat?'

'Did you?'

'You should try a joint with us next time.' He was swaying and smiling. His unkempt hair was falling in his eyes.

'Go back to your boyfriend,' hissed Michael, 'and if I get you in that room again, I'll thump your teeth down your throat. You hear me?'

Still Haddock smiled, and turned and waved each individual finger as he walked drifting back into his own room. Michael stood looking after him, his fists knotted.

When he went back to Owen, the boy was dancing by himself to the music, his head loose and wobbling. Michael grabbed him by the shoulders.

'You're not to let that guy back in here.'

Owen looked hard at him.

'Your face is dirty,' he said. 'And your

hands . . .'

'Do you hear me? You're not to let him in.'

'But I like him,' said Owen. He was groggy.

'That's what he wants you to do.'

'So what's wrong with that?'

'Everything is wrong with it.'

'Whaddyamean?'

'Never mind. Someday I'll explain.' Michael sat down and put his head in his hands.

'Smoking fags is one thing. But Jesus, Owen, *drugs*? Did he touch you?'

'Huh?'

'Did he do anything to you? Will you stop jiving around and sit down and listen. Did he?'

Because the boy looked confused by the question Michael guessed that nothing had happened and he left the subject alone. What he did know was that Haddock would never get another opportunity. He would take the boy away. To leave him all day amongst queers and junkies was asking too much.

'How much did you tell him?'

'Nuthin'.'

'Liar. When you sober up I want to talk to you seriously.'

He made himself a meal but could not eat it. Owen ate half of his but was sick afterwards on the stairs. Michael left it, hoping that Haddock would slip in it.

That night, lying on the mattress, Michael could not sleep. The plan would have to become a reality. If he had the courage.

172

Sacrifice was required. God knows, he had tried every way to avoid it. It was the only answer left.

On the boards above them Keith and Barry squealed and danced to pounding music well into the small hours of the morning, and Michael heard in it the frenzy of the dance of death.

CHAPTER SIXTEEN

The airport lounge echoed with the noise of voices and chimes announcing flights. Michael and Owen walked across to pick up and pay for the tickets he had reserved over the phone. When the girl had asked him what name, without thinking he had given his own, Michael Lamb. He now collected the tickets and checked in his baggage. He had to stuff the transistor into his bag because they would not let him carry it as hand luggage. He remembered Owen's gun at the bottom of the bag and, to save any further questions, he dropped it in the litter bin, saying that he would buy him another. The knife and sheath Owen kept in his inside pocket. They had some time to wait so they wandered round the shops in the airport. Owen found a football magazine section.

'Are you happy enough?' asked Michael. It

was the first words he had spoken to him since the previous day, apart from telling him that they were to fly to Ireland. This was not the way he had planned it. Their last days should have been happy together. At least Owen's should. Michael knew now that he would never be happy in his life again. It was essential that Owen be cosseted, be loved, be happier than he had ever been in his life before. In the taxi to the airport Michael had made the decision to forget totally the Haddock affair. The boy had been a dupe.

And it was necessary for Michael for the first time to deceive him. He must keep up a front. Be kind to be cruel to be kind. The boy must have no hint of what was to happen. Therefore Michael had to be his normal self. He made a truce.

'Owen?'

'What?' He looked up from leafing through a magazine.

'You're O.K.' He ruffled his hair with his hand. The boy smiled and shrugged, embarrassed but glad to be in with him again. 'Now, I'm going a message. I am not running away from you. Stay here and I'll be back in a second.' The boy nodded and before he turned to his magazine again he stuck his tongue out at him. Michael laughed for him.

He found a chemist's and bought a bottle of aspirin and some boiled sweets. He went back to the bookshop and gave Owen a sweet.

174

'Here, suck one of these. It'll stop you being sick on the plane.'

They were well up in the queue when their flight was announced so that they got a window seat behind the wing.

'Have you ever flown before, Mick?'

'No. I'm just as nervous as you.'

He felt ten times worse. His stomach was tight and he felt on the verge of throwing up while the plane was still taxi-ing. It seemed to make the most terrible noise. Then it swung round and faced the long runway. The note of the engines changed to a scream. The whole machine juddered and tilted as if being held back. Then suddenly it rushed forward. Michael felt his insides twist at the unleash of power. The runway was a blur beneath the wing, then it clarified. There was a tree and a road and a field.

'Look. Look,' yelled Owen. 'We're up.'

'Thank God.'

A voice like a razor blade came over the loudspeaker and told them a whole lot of facts about their flight and ended by telling them that they could smoke.

'Hear that?' said Owen.

'Don't be silly,' said Michael and offered him another boiled sweet.

It was a clear day and they could see for miles. Countryside latticed with roads and railway lines. Green and yellow and brown squares. The dark green sludge of forests.

'Jesus, look at the wing,' said Owen. 'It's shaking.'

Michael looked and saw that it was. It was shaking very badly—as if it was going to fall off.

'Not to worry,' he said. He looked round to see if anyone else was panicking. But everyone was calm. 'It must be normal,' he said.

Just then a man came down the plane distributing cards and asking people to fill them in. Michael looked at his. It was to do with security. He felt a flutter of a panic of a different kind. The man passed on. The card asked questions like name, address, purpose of visit, length of stay. Had they any way of checking up if he gave a false name? But he couldn't give a false name because his ticket was in his own name. They would certainly know and check that. He wrote his own name and his father's address, that he was returning from holiday to go on another short holiday in Donegal before returning home. He filled in Owen's for him, calling him Owen Lamb and giving the same information. He sat worrying whether or not this would be good enough.

Michael was kicking himself for having chosen this route. Since yesterday, since he had decided that the plan was to go ahead he was acting as if in a dream. The fugue, indeed. Events since then seemed to float up to him and go past as if he was an observer. It was as if he could not, even if he wanted to, reach out and touch anything. Useless words and phrases stuck in his mind when he didn't want them to. The cadence of the girl in the chemist's. 'Asprin. Very good, sir.' The man distributing cards: 'Just fill this in, sir.' He had forgotten about the amount of security on the Belfast flight. He could have gone to Shannon and up the west to Donegal. He knew the Gardai would have informed the police in the North. Maybe the Troubles would work in his favour. Looking for Provos and forgetting the rest.

'What's wrong?' asked Owen.

'Nothing.'

They moved out over the sea. It was blue and green and translucent. Below them was a beach of yellow sand and they could see it shelving out into deeper and deeper water. Small islands had skirts of brown seaweed and black rocks under the surface.

'Makes you feel like a bird,' said Owen. 'A vulture.'

'Flying in circles.'

Suddenly the plane lurched and began to fall. It seemed to fall horizontally as if there was nothing underneath it.

'Oh Jesus Christ,' said Michael. His stomach ballooned into his mouth. He held with white knuckles on to the arms of his seat. Then the plane stopped falling and it was even worse as it rose again, riding up the air. Michael turned his head towards Owen.

'Fuck me,' said the boy. 'This is desperate.'

The wings seemed to shudder so much that they must fall off. Out of the window the horizon tilted and seemed to go above them. They began to plunge again. Further this time than the last. It seemed to go on for ever. Michael was sure that they must hit the sea. He tried to pray. The plane bucked upwards again. The razor voice came across and apologized for the turbulence. They were trying to fly to a different altitude. The plane began to climb steadily but lost its footing once or twice and plunged again. Eventually they left the air turbulence and Michael settled to worry about the police at the other end. As yet no one had collected the cards, so there wouldn't be time to check all the names. He wondered what they were for.

Owen pulled at his elbow.

'There's Ireland,' he said. Michael leaned across him and looked down. Small dinky fields, much smaller, much greener than the English ones, and the jagged silver of Lough Neagh, big as a sea.

They were asked by the voice to hand the completed cards to the stewardess as they were leaving the plane and to fasten their seat belts.

Passing through Security Michael whispered to Owen, 'Let me hold your hand. It looks better.'

He took the boy's hand in his own and walked straight up to the plain-clothes men flanking the exit door. They stared into the faces of everyone who passed them, picking someone out occasionally for questioning.

Michael and Owen passed through without being stopped. In the lounge Michael heaved a sigh.

'Thank God for that. I need a drink.'

They picked up their bag as it came, its label trembling, along what Owen called the flat moving staircase. Then they made for the bar. Owen reached out his hand and put it in Michael's. Michael held it tightly for a moment. Then let it go.

'It's O.K. There's no need now. It was just to get past the heavies.' Owen shrugged. He seemed offended and thrust his hands in his pockets and did his cowboy walk.

'O.K. Come on.' Michael tried to release the boy's hand from his pocket but Owen pulled away, walking at a distance from him.

After a drink they went to the car hire kiosk and Michael got a car. Again he gambled and used his own name. He had no option because he knew he would have to show his driving licence. The girl, all make-up and uniform, took the details and the money and asked no further questions.

'What colour is it?' asked Owen.

'Red,' said the girl and smiled at him.

On the way to the car Michael took Owen by the hand. A lot of the fight seemed to have gone out of the boy. Michael thought he was becoming pathetic and wanting a little too much attention. Then he felt guilty at the thought, remembering.

In the car they both felt better. Owen could have a cigarette. As they roared along they sang some hymns at the tops of their voices. It was a sort of compromise as Michael knew none of the words of the pop tunes that Owen wanted to sing. They both knew the airs and words of hymns. They sang 'Hail, Glorious St Patrick' and 'Star of the Sea'. After Randalstown it began to rain and the rhythmic swipe of the windscreen wipers made Michael feel sleepy. Owen sat in the front passenger seat, smoking. Earlier they had had a fight about seat belts and Michael had insisted and shouted at the boy. Owen had said that only poofs wore them. Michael had belted him in and the boy had almost chain smoked since, presumably, Michael thought, to prove that he wasn't a poof. Owen kept urging him to pass everything on the road and for a while Michael had played the game, but when the rain came on he stopped taking risks.

'The air in this car is polluted,' said Michael.

'Open a window.'

'And get soaked, just because you want to smoke twenty fags in a row.'

'Six,' said the boy.

The road twisted and turned and plunged out of sight in front of them. Its banks were covered with thick summer foliage, making it seem narrower. To the left behind a hedge it appeared again, squirming its way to the top of a hill.

'Are you hungry?' Michael asked.

'Yeah.'

'Then we'll stop at the next pub we see and get a breath of fresh air. I'm going to die of lung cancer if I stay in here any longer.'

It was some time before they found a place to stop and Michael almost missed it because of the fifteen-foot wire security fence which surrounded it. At the gate they were both searched by an old man who ran his hands lightly over their pockets. Inside Owen whispered that he had missed the knife.

Afterwards, when they got into the car, Owen put on his seat belt without a word of protest. They drove in silence to Strabane. Other towns they had passed through had shown little signs of the Troubles—an occasional burnt-out shop or boarded-up windows. For security reasons they had been rerouted round the fringes of towns and therefore did not see what had happened in the centres.

But in Strabane the evidence was everywhere. Tall terraces of shops with charred rafters for roofs, crumbling gables, slogans sprayed everywhere, men with nothing to do standing sheltering from the rain in doorways. Two or three minutes passing through Strabane in the rain was enough to depress Michael even more than he thought he could be. A town bent on self-destruction. Cutting off its nose to spite the British Government's face. The air was full of a savage and bewildered gloom and Michael drove away from the town with it still clinging to him.

He wanted to tell someone, to justify himself to someone, to say this was the only possible way. Apart from Haddock, he had spoken to no adult since he left. He wondered for a moment if, because of his opting out of the adult world, he had got things out of perspective. But he had always thought that a child saw the world for what it was. Simply, purely and with a sure sense of justice.

'Do you know what will happen if we're caught?' he asked Owen.

'They'll put you inside for a while.'

'No, that doesn't matter. Do you know what'll happen to you?'

'They'll put me back in the Home for ever.'

'How do you fancy that?'

'With Benny?' The boy spewed the name out, making a fish mouth.

'Is that the worst thing that could happen?'

'You bet.'

'I don't bet because I always lose,' said Michael and this time he did not laugh.

They crossed the border into Donegal. The boy became uneasy, fidgeting in his seat. Then he started to ask a question but choked it back.

'What's up?' asked Michael.

'Where are we heading?'

'North.'

'*Away* from the Home?'

'Away from the Home,' said Michael firmly.

The boy relaxed and put his feet up on the dashboard.

'Tonight,' said Michael, 'we'll stay in a hotel somewhere and tomorrow we'll head north to the best beach I know—'

CHAPTER SEVENTEEN

Owen.

Michael woke to the familiar depressing screech of gulls. Before his eyes had opened he knew it was the day. His tongue tasted of copper and he was unsure whether he had slept or not. The pillow was damp at his cheek. He must have slept, for his mouth had dribbled. He did not want to move, to do anything. His eye fixed itself on the plaster fleur-de-lis, out of which the light flex grew, without seeing it. His eye wandered its intricacies without knowing. *Petit mal*. He wondered if this was what it was like, to see, to hear and feel and taste and be incapable of the slightest motion of fingertip or eyelid or lip or tongue. To be at the same time unaware. Hopelessness had paralysed him. The inescapability of the *grand mal* that was to come had cut the nerves that controlled his extremities. He wondered where, all of a sudden, the bits of French had come from. Brother Benedict would have sneered that he was a man with one eye, a cyclops, would have sneered coward at him, would have called him a moral degenerate, with a dismissive and irritated wobble of the back of his hand.

Owen.

When the time came, would he have the strength? Was he capable of such an act? The love he had for the boy would see him through. He knew it. Each morning he was his first waking thought and each night he did not sleep because of him and every hour of the day was absorbed by him down to the creasing of his brow and the bitten half-moons of his fingernails.

He got out of bed and dressed quietly, putting on the T-shirt with Owen's picture on it. In the bathroom he washed his face but avoided looking at himself in the mirror.

Owen Kane.

Michael pulled the curtains and the sun struck hard and bright across the room, making Owen's eyes wince and retract almost beneath his brows. He muttered and turned his back to the light. Michael told him softly that it was time to get up, and turned to the window. The wasteland of Donegal, tweed green fading into brown, fading in the pale blue of the mountains, uninterrupted by trees of any sort. A place without shelter. He told the boy he would wait for him in the dining room.

They ate a breakfast of bacon, egg and sausage and fried soda bread. Although it was home-made food served by a family, different from anything they had eaten in England, Michael found it tasteless, requiring to be chewed too much before he could risk swallowing it. The previous night they had hunted for a hotel, but they were all booked up so they had to make do with a bed and breakfast place. Owen said that he preferred it to any hotel they had stayed in.

The owner's daughters served the breakfast, two lovely girls in bright dresses and aprons, about Owen's age. They were shy and smiling, bringing plates of cornflakes and toast, and when Michael said something in praise of them so that they could overhear it, they ran the last few steps out of the room, their pony-tails bouncing. When they had finished their meal and the girls had cleared the table with downcast eyes, the mother came in, her forearms bare and folded, to see if everything had been to their liking. The girls came to listen and look at the visitors from the shelter of their mother. Owen was embarrassed to be looked at so he asked Michael if he could go out and play, pointedly calling him Dad in front of the woman and her daughters.

Owen.

In Gaelic Owen meant lamb. Benedict had told him when he said that their stars were crossed.

Michael went up to their room and locked the door. Owen's tablets stood on a small table beside his bed. He opened the wardrobe, put his hand in his jacket pocket and took out the blue bottle of aspirin. He emptied Owen's tablets into the palm of his hand and counted them. He counted out the same number of aspirin and funnelled them, with his hand hinged, into the Epilim bottle. There was a fractional difference in size but it was almost impossible to notice. The Epilim tablets he threw down the sink, flushing them away with the straw-coloured Donegal tap water. After the fry he felt thirsty—as if he was going to be sick—and he took from the metal ring its cradled glass, filled it and drank, hoping the water would be a cure. As he drank his eyes came across himself in the mirror with his lower teeth bared, animal-like and distorted by the refraction of the glass. He spat the dregs into the washbasin and remained head down for some minutes.

He sat down on Owen's bed and tried to steady himself. He heard a fissling noise beneath him and wondered what it was. He stripped back the sheets and saw a large polythene bag laid flat between the sheet and the mattress. The boy must have got it out of the wardrobe. There were coathangers and polythene bags for dust covers lying at the bottom.

There was something about this, this finding what the boy had done without the presence of Owen himself to justify or explain it, that brought him to the verge of tears. A rearrangement of the world, however slight, which was Owen's idea. A mark which had come about unknown to Michael and which the boy did *not* want him to know of. Like coming across a site where a child had secretly played house and has had to leave it with pebbles outlining the walls, hearth, fireplace, flowers.

He knew he must not break. He left the polythene bag where it was and went downstairs, the tablets making a faint rattle in his pocket. The boy was playing outside on the gravel path, trying to lob stones into the mouth of a cement mixer at the side of the house. Every house in Donegal seemed to be adding an extension. Michael offered him the bottle and told him that he had forgotten to take his tablet. When he asked for water, Michael sent him to the kitchen. Owen was reluctant because of the girls. When they had booked into the house the woman had given them a cup of tea and a large wedge of chocolate cake. The girls had smiled through the serving hatch and Owen said that they looked as if they were on television.

The boy came out from the kitchen with a red face. Michael asked him which of them he wanted to marry and Owen tried to punch him, but Michael put his hand on the boy's head and kept him at arm's length so that he was flailing the air. Seeing he could not hit Michael, he stopped and did his cowboy walk to the bench seat at the front of the house and sat down. When Michael went to him he jumped up and said that he had to go upstairs for a minute and not to go away without him, that he had forgotten something. Michael wanted to say something about the girls making the beds but choked it back. This day should be without teasing, it must be different without seeming to be different.

He went and paid the bill and assured the woman that if they were ever back this way again, that this is where he would stay. The woman and the two girls came to the door to wave them off while the father, who had begun mixing cement, paused and took off his cap—a gesture which reminded Michael with a flutter of panic of a greeting reserved for passing funerals.

They drove north towards the Atlantic with the sun shining towards where they could see the taut line of its horizon cradled between two mountains. His hands were moist on the steering wheel so that he had to rub them on his trousers and his mouth was dry. He could think of nothing to say to the boy, and yet he wanted to say everything. For a ludicrous moment he thought he might get him to agree to the whole thing. He found himself looking in the mirror more often than usual to see if there was anyone following them but the road ribboned empty behind them into the distance. Since they had got into the car he had a strange feeling of being watched, of another presence and it wasn't a ghost feeling or a spied-upon feeling, just an aura that they were not alone.

They stopped in a village at the foot of the mountain to buy a picnic. The bed and breakfast had cost less than he expected so he had seven pounds left. He told the boy he could pick anything he liked and Owen chose a giant-size packet of marsh-mallows, some bananas and apples, an angel cake layered with three different colours of sponge and, as a concession to Michael's raised eyebrows and the constant reminders of what sweet things did to your teeth, a tin of sardines. Michael bought rolls and sliced ham, some cheese and a bottle of red wine. Then another bottle of red wine. He asked for a cork-screw and a knife, but when Owen reminded him that he still had his sheath knife, he put the knife back on the counter. He gathered the stuff in his arms and was moving towards the door when the boy whispered that he needed cigarettes and matches.

They travelled on roads cutting across the peat bogs, and tiny figures in white shirts leaned on their spades and took the opportunity for a rest, watching the red car crawl across the landscape. He felt small and ant-like shouldered by the mountains. He could see where he wanted to go between the blue hills, the cleft that would take him through, and yet he knew it would be a long time before he reached it. He saw themselves as if from above, inching across the land, following the dog-legged roads. A bird's-eye view. And yet he knew that this was not a true interpretation of what was happening, or of what was to happen. A bird's-eye view does not see the truth. He could explain if he had the words. Owen accused him of being quiet and he replied that he had not noticed.

They were now between tiny fields cleared of stones, which had been woven into the walls surrounding them. They came down a valley and turned a corner and saw the sea. Owen shouted with delight. It spread out before them blue-grey to its bar at the tight horizon. White breakers toppled and smashed themselves on to rocks by the road. Owen rolled down his window and sniffed the air and Michael told him that it was far better for him than smoking. He warned him not to get too excited, seeing the light in the boy's face. They came to a fork in the road and Michael hesitated, not clearly remembering the way. The signpost gave him no indication, only town names he vaguely recalled. He took the fork nearest the sea and after about two miles saw the domes of sandhills.

Michael parked the car and, laden with their picnic, they moved into the dunes overlooking the beach. The grass was sharp and spiky and Owen kept cursing as it penetrated the cloth of his jeans. They found the last dune before the flatness of the beach and lay down on its shoreward side. As Michael lay back on the dry soft sand the sun came out harshly bright but not warm. Owen, too, nuzzled into the sand, swiping his arms and legs up and down and indicating to Michael that he had made angels' wings. Michael told him to lie down and take it easy, but Owen was full of energy. He ran up the sand dunes, slowing half way up as the sand silted knee-deep, and after grunting his way to the top ran and jumped, ankles cocked, arms above his head, plummeting into the drift of sand some ten feet below. He squealed and whooped with the exhilaration of the fall. After he had done this about four times he came panting back to Michael and lay down beside him, his rib cage heaving. For a time the boy did not say anything, letting his breath return slowly to normal. Michael, his face to the sun, had his eyes closed and when he noticed the boy's silence he jerked his neck up and looked at him to see if he was all right. Then he asked him to tell him again about the feeling he got before one of his bad attacks but the boy refused. Michael was disappointed. He wanted to hear again the boy say that he experienced his weird happiness, wanted to hear him in his groping attempts to describe his ecstasy. He wanted to compare it to what was bound to happen if he did not do what he had planned. Brother Benedict's triumph, his punishments and victimization; the boy's mother weeping and drinking and hating, neither of them appreciating the goodness that was in the boy. Smothering. A life of misery, of frustration that led to inevitable crime and lovelessness, in his own, Michael's absence, stretched into the future. What he planned was for love; what he planned was a photograph, a capturing of the stillness of the moment of the boy's happiness. Irreversible and therefore eternal—if eternity existed. Fortunate in its timeliness. But the boy was silent and Michael deprived of his reassurance. A little rivulet of sand came streaming slowly down from the top of the dune, a dislodged trickle. Michael lowered his voice to a whisper and climbed to the top but he could see no one. The wind made a noise in his ears and when he put his head above the level of the dune the grasses whisked dryly. Owen came up and joined him and they stood together looking at the vast empty stretch of sand, stretching for about two miles, white flat sand fading into rocks at the far end. Except for themselves and a few gulls the beach was completely deserted.

Michael asked him if he would like a swim.

'Oh, Mick, you beaut. Do you mean it?'

'Why not? I'll go in with you, in case.'

'Shit. No togs,' said Owen.

'Go in your drawers. There's nobody about.'

They both stripped to their Y-fronts and ran, arching their feet against the hard ribbed sand near the water. Owen stopped at his ankles.

'Jeeziz, it's freezing,' he yelled. Michael ploughed on out, then flung himself into the arch of an oncoming wave. He swam about for a bit, watching Owen. The boy was standing knee-deep, holding his elbows, his teeth chattering. Michael shouted to him but no amount of coaxing could get him deeper than his knees. The boy backed out and began sprinting across the shallow water parallel to the incoming waves. Michael went to him.

'If you run like this—fast—and look over your shoulder, you think somebody's splashing after you,' screamed Owen. 'He's catching up. He's catching up.' He was running full tilt, looking behind him. Then he must have planted his leading foot badly for he went sprawling in an inch of water and sand. Michael ran to him and picked him up.

'Oh, fyeuch,' said the boy. An emulsion of brown sand and water covered his bony chest and thighs. Michael washed him down with handfuls of sea water, the boy screaming at the cold, and he ran him, all angles and bones, back to the warmth of the sand dune. Through his uncontrollable shiverings Owen said shakily,'I haven't missed much. What the hell was everybody talking about?'

Michael noticed that he had got some black oil on his fingers and he tried to rub it off on the sand. He used his shirt to dry the boy and told him to take off his drawers and leave them to dry in the sun. Owen turned his back to pull on his jeans and again Michael saw the scar marks, now red with cold, across the backs of his legs, the tiny buttocks like eggs. It was as if he saw everything now in a fit of stunned awareness. The helpless, most vivid-of-all moments before a car smash, etched in adrenaline, the slowness. The ability to tease out afterwards each strand of the event. He knew he would not forget an instant of this day, these hours. For some reason he recalled his dread of the steel ball thumping hollowly into the depths of the pinball machine, the inevitability of it despite the frantic flicking of the small rubber wings unable to reach. He felt himself funnelled towards the act he had decided upon, but prayed to God that something would arrest it—even at the last moment.

They had their picnic and Owen drank some wine to warm him. Michael had most of it. He watched the boy closely as he ate, the bitten fingernails pulling the bread into pieces, the half-open mouth as he chewed. Since they had left the bed and breakfast place he had had a great urge to weep, to tell the boy how much he meant to him. Several times, when they brushed together, especially at the water's edge after he had fallen, he nearly did so, but he controlled himself for the boy's sake. He must know nothing, suspect nothing if it was to be perfect; if the ecstasy was to be there. So Michael held back because it would be selfish not to. He reminded Owen it was tablet time again and the boy took one, washing it down with wine, making a face. The sun disappeared into a cloud and the whole sky began to cover over. The cloud was low, cutting off the tops of the mountains. Crushing down. Michael suggested they go for a walk to warm themselves, so they put on shoes. Leaning back on their heels, they walked down the steepness of the slope to the flat beach. Michael put his arm around Owen's shoulders and for the length of the walk neither of them spoke. Several times Michael looked over his shoulder and scanned the length of the horizon, but nothing moved. They sat in the lee of a dune for a rest.

He sat facing the boy, watching him, trying to take in every detail of him. The boy's hair had grown blonder and he wondered why he had not noticed it before. He wanted to reach out and touch him but he could think of no excuse for doing so. Out of the corner of his eye something flickered. He turned but there was nothing. The clouds had darkened to the colour of slate and now covered the whole sky.

It had become warmer and Michael felt his hand damp where it had lain on the boy's shoulder. Something flickered again and this time he definitely knew what it was. He drew Owen's attention to the lightning. But the boy seemed not to care, had lost interest; saying that he was tired now, he lay back in the sand. The lightning flashed but there was no thunder. Summer lightning. Michael joked that he shouldn't take so much out of himself in future, but Owen did not hear what he said. His eyes were fixed in front of him. His body went still, then rigid. His left arm gave two little flicks, then his left foot began to quiver. Michael closed his eyes, almost in relief that it had finally happened, and went to him. He put his arms around him and held him tight. In his convulsions the boy churned up the sand and Michael held him as best he could. Then he lifted him, one arm behind his neck, the other in the crook of his knees, and carried him, jerking and flapping and awkward, to the sea where the rocks jagged out to form pools. Michael waded in between the rocks, knelt down and lowered Owen into the water. The child threshed to the surface and Michael had to put his hand on his forehead to keep it under. His wedding ring glinted yellow in the water. The boy's clothes ballooned out, full of air. His own face stared at him from the boy's T-shirt with a look of disbelief. Big bubbles wobbled out of Owen's mouth. His face was blue from the fit. 'Oh Jesus, if you are there, help me.' Michael looked away and up to the sky, away from the boy's face, and saw the lightning flash from clouds rumpled and coloured like brains. His wrists were frozen and a wave almost overbalanced him. He closed his eyes and remembered his teeth refracted in the glass, the old priest's phlegmy cough bubbling in his chest, Benedict drying between his toes. In his gripping fingers he could feel the throb of the boy's life still and he gritted his teeth, willing himself to complete what he had started. He dared to look at Owen's face again. Gradually his fit stopped until there was no movement. The child's hair unfurled, flowing outwards and upwards. He lifted him out of the water dripping and cold and pressed his head to his face. Their skins slid together. He asked the boy to forgive him and told him how much he loved him. Suddenly there was a gasp of breath torn from the bottom of the child's lungs, a ripped-out exhalation of a harshness that was almost a shout and Michael bit blood into his lips as he lowered him into the water again. He began to cry and did not know whether the shudder was his crying or the life of the boy. 'Dear Jesus, make it now.' Again he held him under, amazed at the strange flatness of his white hands and fingers pressing on the underwater flatness of Owen's body. Tiny bubbles had gathered in the child's hair, making it seem like glass or silver, making it rise to the surface. He willed him to die. His neck was thin to the touch, like a wrist, his eyes wide beneath the water with gasping. He realized that the noise which he heard he was making himself, grunting and panting with effort, a strange inarticulate and uninterrupted groaning, too high-pitched, he thought, to be coming from himself. He stopped it and there was silence except for the sea and the gulls. Owen was stilled completely and began to slew back and forth with the waves. Again Michael lifted him out and crushed his head to his own. The child's hands dangled limp from his wrist. His mouth hung open. Michael carried him up the beach away from the tide and laid him on the sand. He pulled his T-shirt straight and put his feet together. With one finger and the palm of his hand he combed the child's yellow hair into place, flattening it, making it look better.

'O.K.,' he said, still crying. 'O.K.'

Then he ran stumbling back to the water, in a strange high-stepping gait so that the water would not impede him. Waist-deep he waded, moving his shoulders like Owen's cowboy walk. He closed his eyes, remembering, and flung himself face forward into the water, but it was too ·shallow, his trailing hands knuckled the sandy bottom and he stood up again spluttering, wiping his mouth, brushing water from his beard and waded out further. But the incline of the beach was too shallow. He knew it was ludicrous and inappropriate to feel so, but what he felt was foolishness. After the first plunge, when he arose he looked around to see if anyone had seen him. He stood stirring the icy water with his hands and then he closed his eyes and again fell forward on his face, the water enveloping him. It gurgled in his ears and he held his breath. He began to count but did not want to count; seven, eight, nine, ten; he opened his mouth, eleven, twelve, and inhaled through his nose and immediately began to splutter and regurgitate what he had swallowed. At the same time he floundered and a wave caught him and carried him shoreward and he splashed to his feet again, his hands clawing and springing back off the sand, and he came out of the water in a thresh of foam, coughing and spitting. He was on his knees, chest-deep. His hair covered his eyes and was stuck flat. He remained like that for some time, listening to the water around him. Eventually he pushed his hair back, stood up and walked back, retching, to ankle-depth. His clothes clung to him, heavy and dark with the water, and with his head bowed he moved away from the water's edge—past the place where Owen lay. Water bubbled from the lace holes in his shoes with the pressure of each step. He could not bear to look at the boy again. In the sandhills he crouched, his arms encircling his knees to stop them shivering. He did not know how long for. His flesh was goose-flesh. Long enough for him to dry. He had no luck. No faith. And now, no love. He had started with a pure loving simple ideal but it had gone foul on him, turned inevitably into something evil. It had been like this all his life, with the Brothers, with the very country he came from. The beautiful fly with the hook embedded. It was engrained like oil into the whorls and loops of his fingertips. The good that I do is the evil that results. He tasted the bitterness in his mouth. Whether it was the blood of his lips or the salt of the sea or the tears he was crying, he did not know or care. Owen was dead. He had killed him to save him, although he loved him more than anyone else in his life. He felt gutted. It was as if his insides and his soul had been burned out. There was nothing left of him but the sound of his crying. He looked up, even though he did not want to look up, even though he could not bear to look, and saw the child in the distance like a flaw on the sand and about him cruising and hovering he saw three gulls, their yellow beaks angled with screeching, descending slowly, with meticulous care.